DRAUGHT OF DEATH

Edward Dawson, a distinguished professor, has been found drowned in a vat of beer in the brewery where he carried out his research. The pathologist is convinced he was murdered and when Sergeant Bragg and Constable Morton of the City of London begin to investigate it appears that Dawson was an inveterate philanderer who also had many rivals in academic circles. Bragg and Morton's enquiries uncover serious academic malpractice and bitter boardroom rivalries, before reaching a surprising conclusion.

DRAUGHT OF DEATH

DRAUGHT OF DEATH

DRAUGHT OF
DEATH

by

Ray Harrison

Dales Large Print Books
Long Preston, North Yorkshire,
BD23 4ND, England.

British Library Cataloguing in Publication Data.

Harrison, Ray
    Draught of death

      A catalogue record of this book is
      available from the British Library

      ISBN   1-84137-009-6 pbk

First published in Great Britain by Constable & Company Ltd., 1998

Copyright © 1998 by Ray Harrison

Cover illustration by arrangement with Constable & Company Ltd.

Published in Large Print 2000 by arrangement with Constable &
Company Ltd.

Dales Large Print is an imprint of Library Magna Books Ltd.

Printed and bound in Great Britain by
T.J. (International) Ltd., Cornwall, PL28 8RW

To Tony and Sylvie King.

1

Detective Sergeant Joseph Bragg, of the City of London police, finished spraying the last rose bush. It was a waste of time, he thought. Every June that he had lodged with Mrs Jenks the greenfly had smothered the buds, and black blotches had covered the leaves. What else could she expect, with all these coal fires spewing smoke and ash around? Now, in the Dorset village of his boyhood, you really could grow roses! Five inches across, some of them... Not that he had grown roses himself. In truth, he had never been much more than a potterer in his father's garden. And that had been down to vegetables, not flowers. And they had to take their chance most years... His father had owned a small carter's business. His busiest time came just as the garden needed work on it. Many a time Bragg had been faced with clearing weeds a foot high, instead of hanging around at the crossroads whistling after the girls.

Perhaps he should be grateful. When he went down to Turner's Puddle nowadays, he wondered how anybody could be content in the country. Back-breaking toil, punctuated by leaning on a gate watching the grass grow. He had certainly been lucky. A big strapping lad, his father had allowed him to drive one of the small wagons. And him no more than eleven years old! He would be up at five on a summer morning; feed and water the horse, then walk to Dorchester with a load of hay – all of ten miles before breakfast. No wonder it had palled! At fourteen he had persuaded his father to let him take a job in a shipping office in Weymouth. There he was, barely scraping by in the three Rs, suddenly confronted by bills of lading, invoices, manifests, accounts. It had been a bit of a facer, but he had stuck at it. And it came in handy now, to know his way around a set of business books. But for that, he might still be on the beat.

Not that he had long to go anyway. In a year's time he would be forty-five; over the hill, pensioned off. He wondered what they would have done, had his wife lived. She had kept her end up against the towny wives, when they were living in the married quarters. And, when the baby was on the way, she had been over the moon! That they should both be mucked away by inept midwives... A breech birth, they said; nothing could be done... They had shrugged their collective shoulders, and turned to the next case.

He tried to force his thoughts into a happier channel. Amy and Fanny Hildred were coming up from Dorset – indeed, would have reached London by now. It looked as if Amy was at last coming round to selling their brewery. Since her husband's death, she had kept it going as if it were a sacred trust. More than kept it going; it was thriving – enough for a London brewery to want to buy it. And the longer the negotiations went on, the more he might see of Fanny. On his visits to Bere Regis, to stay with his cousin, she had seemed to seek him out. Since his last visit, they had kept up a desultory correspondence. Letters which

Mrs Jenks would place by his plate with a disapproving sniff. Life was odd. Here he was, just turned forty-four, and thinking of young women ... or one not-so-young woman. A good ten years younger than him, probably. Not past child-bearing for a few years yet. Perhaps he ought to trim his moustache a bit, before they met. It was looking a bit ragged.

'Mr Bragg! Mr Bragg!' Mrs Jenks was screeching at him through the window. 'There's a policeman here wants you!'

'Bugger!'

'Now, that's enough of that!... He says it's urgent.'

'All right, I'm coming.' Bragg picked up the bucket, and threw the remaining spray over the sweet peas. At least they would stay clear of pests for a bit.

A young constable with gleaming boots was standing in the hallway. On seeing Bragg he came to attention.

'Message from the desk sergeant, sir,' he said crisply.

'You new, son?' Bragg asked.

'Yes, sir.'

'Ex-army?'

'Yes, sir. Royal Fusiliers.'

'Well, cut out the parade-ground antics, and we'll get along fine.'

'Sir!... There has been a death at Tyrrell's brewery, off Tudor Street. Someone drowned in a vat.'

'I see.'

'The sergeant said it might suit you, whatever that means.'

'It means I have been known to have an occasional pint, lad; nothing more... Right, I will pop round and see what it is all about.'

'You won't need me, then?'

'No. But, if I were you, I wouldn't rush back to Old Jewry. I'd have a wander round the streets; get to know them a bit. Once you are on the beat, you will see nothing but your own patch... Married, are you?'

'Yes, sir.' He smiled warmly. 'Living in the married quarters ... fallen on my feet, I reckon!'

'Good! What's your name, son?'

'Rodgers, sir.'

'Keep your nose clean, Rodgers, and you might make the detective division one day.'

13

The constable grinned. 'I'd like that – Sherlock Holmes, eh?'

Bragg frowned. 'No, not Sherlock bloody Holmes! Long hours and hard graft; and precious little thanks from the City fathers.'

Rodgers's grin faded. 'Right, sir... Then, I'll report back to Old Jewry.'

'Do that, lad.'

Bragg closed the door behind him with a sigh. He shouldn't have bitten the man's head off like that; particularly as he was a new recruit. There was always a bit of needle between the detective division and the uniformed police. But there had been no call to add to it. If he were honest, he would admit that he had been hoping to avoid any involvement in a case, while Fanny and her mother were in London. He had told the desk sergeant as much. Then, that was behind the remark that it would suit him. He had been tipped the wink that he could spin it out.

Bragg walked briskly towards the centre of the City, then waved down a hansom in Cornhill. The streets here were deserted on a Saturday afternoon, and the cab trotted easily along. But coming up to St Paul's there was the usual crowd of trippers. He wondered if Fanny had ever been round the cathedral. It would be somewhere to take her, if he got the chance. An innocent wander around its cool echoing vastness... But perhaps that was not the right note to strike. Something more worldly might be better. Take her to a real cockney pub, for oysters and stout. But how would her mother react to that? On the face of it, she could only approve. After all, their wealth had come from brewing beer... It was strange that he would be working on a case involving the very brewery that was negotiating to buy Hildred's. An omen? He roused himself as the cab turned into Tudor Street, and set him down outside the brewery.

The smell was encouraging anyway, Bragg thought; yeasty, hoppy, malty. It was a good long time since he had drunk Tyrrell's beer. Time to put that right... Once through the gate he found himself in a large cobbled yard. On three sides was a jumble of buildings; some of stone, most of soot-blackened brick. A great chimney towered above the works, smoke drifting lazily from it on the light breeze. At its base, clouds of steam were spurting from a valve in the boiler house. Everything seemed to be on a gigantic scale. The roof ridge of the highest building must be approaching a hundred feet above ground level. To his right, a dray was being loaded with barrels. An ostler was harnesssing a pair of splendid shire horses to it; massive beasts, with the temperament of a pet pony. They talked of the industrial revolution, but steam lorries and petrol engines would never take their place.

He grabbed the arm of a passing workman. 'Who is in charge here?' he asked.

'I am, at the moment. Why?'

'Sergeant Bragg, of the City police. I gather you have a foreign body in your beer.'

The man frowned. 'Oh, he's English all right,' he said. 'Something to do with the college.'

'And what is your name, sir?'

'Dick ... Dick White. I'm a foreman. All the bosses are off, it being Saturday afternoon.'

'Right, Dick. Tell me what happened.'

The foreman scratched his head. 'I can't rightly say. This bloke can come and go as he pleases. I never knew he was here, till one of the lads happened to go into the old vat house, and saw his boots sticking out over the side of the vat.'

'Where is the body?'

'We got it down, and put it on a stretcher. It's still there.'

'In the vat house?'

'Yes.'

'Take me there, will you?'

The foreman led the way across the yard and into one of the buildings. Along its walls were the towering columns of great vats. Ten of them, around fifty feet high.

'Hold four thousand gallons each, they do,' the foreman said, noting Bragg's astonishment.

'I am surprised you could see his feet up there!'

'No! It wasn't here. This is the new vat house, built in the 1840s.'

'So fifty years is new in the brewing trade, is it?'

'It is, when you think that the old vat house was built in 1767 – or so the date-stone says... Come through here.'

Bragg followed him through a doorway into a smaller building. On one wall was a vat that Bragg guessed was thirty feet high; to its right was a smaller one, say fourteen feet. Two ladders were propped against the wall. By the smaller vat was a stretcher, on which lay the sodden body of a man. Foam flecked his clothes and hair, his eyes were staring emptily. Bragg put his age at mid-forties.

'You say he was found in the small vat. When was this?'

'Less than an hour ago.'

'And he has something to do with University College?'

'That's right. He's a professor there ... or was. He used to come experimenting. That was the only reason we kept the small vat going, really.'

There was a commotion outside, then a burly man in his fifties burst in. He strode over to the stretcher and stared at the body. Then he looked up at Bragg.

'You are the policeman, I take it,' he said brusquely.

'That's right, sir. Sergeant Bragg. It's a nice change for us to be called in straight away.'

'My name is Lubbock. I am the chief brewer here.'

'Who is the dead man?'

Lubbock sighed irritably. 'Professor Dawson, of University College London. He has been doing research on certain types of wort-spoilers. The board decided to give him the run of the place, thinking it would be good for business. Now look what has happened!'

'And, who would know he was going to be here?'

'No one, sergeant. He would come and go as the whim took him... Did you find him, Dick?'

The foreman shook his head. 'Jack Thompson found him. I thought it best to get him out, in case he was still alive. When we decided he was dead, I felt we should send for the police.'

'So I see.'

19

'What form did his research take?' Bragg asked. 'What was he actually doing when he came here?'

Lubbock frowned. 'Beer can get infected in the brewing. Bugs and wild yeasts can get into the wort. It being warm, they grow there rapidly. The brew starts stinking of rotting vegetation... It doesn't happen as often as it did when I started here. But, when it happens, by God you know about it!'

'And, who would be aware of his work, apart from you?'

'Well, he has had a couple of students here. They have been working on their own account, I think. But he seemed to keep an eye on what they were doing.'

Bragg took out his notebook. 'Can you give me their names, sir?' he asked.

'The first one was Turnbury ... Roger Turnbury, I think. The current one is a lad called David Waller.'

'Do you have addresses for them?'

'No. The college would tell you, I expect.'

'Right. Have you any idea where Dawson lived?'

Lubbock took out a notebook and began to leaf through the pages. 'Here we are,' he said at length, 'Bedford Square, Bloomsbury – number eight.'

'Right. Is he married, do you know?'

'Yes.'

'Then, I will go and break the news. Leave the body as it is. I will call in at the mortuary, and get them to collect it.'

Lubbock frowned. 'There is no question but that it was an accident, surely?' he said.

'Looks that way, sir. But we must go through the motions ... I expect you will have to get rid of that brew now, won't you?'

'Whyever should we do that?'

'Well, you don't know how long the body's been there. And, at a certain stage after death, the bladder voids itself. So that beer could be spoiled.'

Lubbock snorted. 'There are some sects, in India, that regularly drink their own urine! Of course, I shall report to the other directors on the matter. After all, the loss of two thousand gallons of finished beer is as nothing, if a sergeant of police is worried about a pint of pee!'

Once he had arranged for the mortuary van to collect Dawson's body, Bragg took a cab to Bloomsbury. Eight, Bedford Square was the end house of an elegant terrace. This was an upper-class area, and no mistake; the square laid out with lawns and trees. You could barely hear the traffic, when you were standing at the front door. One thing was certain: you had to have money – sacks of it – to live in a place like this. Would a professor's salary stretch to it? He rang the bell, and turned to gaze over the gardens. It must be one of the best addresses in the whole of London... The door was opened by a smart young maid.

'I would like to have a word with Mrs Dawson, please,' he said.

The girl cocked her head. 'She's not in,' she said.

'Do you know where she might be?'

'No. And if I did, I wouldn't go telling any Tom, Dick and Harry where she was.'

Bragg showed her his warrant-card 'City police,' he said. 'Are you on the telephonic system here?'

22

The girl smiled. 'Yes, we are,' she said proudly.

'Then, will you ask Mrs Dawson to ring the Old Jewry police station, as soon as she gets back?'

She frowned, then nodded.

'By the way, can you find the address of one of Professor Dawson's colleagues? Name of Waller.'

'You had better come into the sitting-room.'

She led the way into a ground-floor room overlooking the square. A large knee-hole desk was in the centre of a rich Turkey carpet. The window was draped with heavy velvet curtains; on either side of the fireplace were large mahogany bookcases. The maid went over to a side-table on which a telephone instrument stood. She took an address-book from a drawer and leafed through its pages.

'Are you sure I should be telling you this?' she asked. 'Only I don't want to get into trouble.'

Bragg smiled. 'You needn't worry. Professor Dawson will never know, I promise you.'

'All right. There is only one Waller here; so it must be him, mustn't it?'

'What does it say?'

'Number three, Bowling Green Lane, Clerkenwell.'

'I see.' Bragg jotted down the address. 'Now, you won't forget to tell Mrs Dawson to ring us, will you?'

'I won't forget.'

Clerkenwell was a far cry from Bedford Square, Bragg thought. Bowling Green Lane sounded countrified – trim lawns and gravelled paths. But the reality was soot-stained, mean houses and broken pavements. His knock was answered by a young woman. She was clutching a handkerchief; her eyes were red-rimmed.

'Am I right in thinking a David Waller lodges here?' he asked in a reassuring voice.

She sniffed. 'Yes, he does.'

'Is he in?'

'No.'

'I see... Would you know where he is?'

'When he's not here, he is usually in the library at University College.'

'Thank you... That's a nasty cold you've got, miss. Always seem worse in the summer, somehow.'

'Yes. Mind you don't catch it!' She banged the door shut.

Interesting, Bragg thought, as he turned away. Still, girls of her age were apt to cry at nothing... What would she be? Early twenties? Should have got past the mawkish stage.

Catherine Marsden turned into Furnival's Inn and walked towards Woods Hotel. It was surprising that the Hildreds would choose such an establishment to stay in. It was a haunt of commercial travellers, and businessmen of only modest pretensions. It did not have a lift, and Catherine was forced to walk up four flights of stairs to reach the room they occupied. The door was opened by Fanny.

'Mamma is out,' she said warmly. 'So we shall be able to have a lovely long chat. I was delighted to hear of your engagement to James Morton! He is such a fine young man.'

Catherine smiled. 'At least I think so ... though sometimes I wonder about his motives for proposing.'

'Why?' Fanny asked in a shocked voice. 'He has been devoted to you for years!'

'I suspect that he may have a passion for tidiness. You know, of course, that his elder brother died at the end of April.'

'Is it two months already? How this summer is flying by!'

'Not for James, I assure you! At last there is, now, not even a theoretical possibility that he will not succeed to the baronetcy. Having kept him at arm's length all these years, his father has begun to involve him in matters concerning the family estates. Welcomed him back into the fold. I sometimes suspect that his proposing may have been merely a step in this dynastic realignment. The new heir ensuring that he can beget an heir of his own.'

'That sounds exceedingly cynical!' Fanny exclaimed. 'You are teasing me, surely.'

'Perhaps. However, things did not go entirely as he wished. Or, indeed, as I would have wished. My godmother, Lady Lanesborough, pointed out an obvious difficulty. In my delight and – I confess it – relief that James had proposed, I had not given the matter a moment's thought.'

'You are speaking in riddles!' Fanny exclaimed.

'Am I? Sorry! I seem to be bubbling with excitement half the time! I am sure that the editor of the *City Press* is going to admonish me for undue levity in my articles!'

'But that would hardly concern you, surely, if you are to be married?'

'Oh, but it would! James and I are going to continue with our careers, after we are married.'

'Do you not want children?'

Catherine smiled. 'Oh, yes! But not yet. And it is possible to postpone a family, in these enlightened days.'

'So wherein lies the difficulty?'

'We shall have to put off our wedding for a year.'

'A year!' Fanny exclaimed. 'Why on earth must you do that?'

'In the social set to which my family belongs – and James's also – there are very strict rules of conduct. They are not always logical, or even defensible, but they are set in stone. You flout them at your peril.'

'I would hardly think that getting married would count as antisocial conduct!'

'No. But it is decreed that the ladies of a family must wear black for twelve months, after a bereavement.'

'That is universal, even if it is not always observed.'

'Yes. But there is a corollary to it. In society, ladies may not go to a wedding wearing black. Since James's mother and sister must be in mourning for a year after Edwin's death, they would not be able to come to our wedding during that period. So it must perforce be postponed... As you can imagine, James was furious about it; so much so that I almost relented. It is no more valid than empty piety, I admit. But, if you want to belong to a tribe, you have to abide by its customs. And I do not wish to be an outcast. So wait we must!'

'Until next April?'

'In the event, until May. We are going to erect a marquee in Hyde Park, opposite our house, for the reception. It will be a highlight of the Season – at least for me! I do hope you will come.'

'You would invite me?' Fanny exclaimed incredulously.

'Of course! James and I must have some real friends at our wedding. Most of the guests will be relatives and society luminaries. And of the rest, a good number will be people whose portraits my father has painted – or hopes to paint!'

'You are very generous,' Fanny exclaimed. 'And I would love to be there... But I would know no one. And I am rather out of my depth in London.'

Catherine smiled. 'At least you will know one other of our special guests. I think Constable Morton will persuade Sergeant Bragg to suspend his pursuit of villains for long enough to see us married!'

Fanny felt a blush rising to her cheeks. 'Why, yes, I do know Sergeant Bragg. Indeed, he has invited me to go to the theatre with him, this evening. Mother will be immersed in the complexities of selling the brewery... In some ways I wish that

Tyrrell's had not approached her. She has so much energy and determination, that life without purpose, without a challenge, would be unbearable to her.'

'She could immerse herself in good works,' Catherine suggested.

Fanny smiled. 'I doubt if the recipients of her charity would enjoy being dragooned into an acceptable degree of gratitude!' she said. 'Now, something much more important! May I see your engagement ring?'

'Alas! I dare not wear it at the moment. I find it is a little loose on my finger. It would be a disaster, were I to pull it off with my glove. So it will have to go back to the jeweller. But you shall see it tomorrow.'

There came a rattle at the door, and a red-faced, stocky woman marched in. 'London is much too hot for Christians,' she pronounced in a commanding voice. 'Ah, Miss Marsden! Nice to see you ... I do not know how you can bear such weather – so airless and humid!'

Catherine smiled. 'I suppose we Londoners get used to it.'

'Of course, you live on Hyde Park! These stupid men at Tyrrell's assumed that we would be content with this dreary doss-house. I do not care that it is convenient for the brewery! We want to go round the shops while we are here.'

'Naturally!'

'When I expressed my dissatisfaction, the wretched Tyrrell people intimated that they were going to pay the bill – as if that was ample justification... Can you suggest any acceptable alternative, Miss Marsden?'

'Not in the City – or indeed anywhere close to it... How long do you expect to be in London?'

Amy frowned. 'It depends on the course of these negotiations. I am reconciled to selling the brewery. I shall not go on for ever. And Fanny shows neither desire nor aptitude for running it. Since I am a woman, Tyrrell's board thought they had only to mention a half-decent price and I would jump at it. But my husband spent his life building up the business. I will not fritter it away! I could go on for years yet.'

'But you are unlikely to be in London for

more than another week or so,' Catherine said. 'In which case you might find the St James's Hotel both convenient and pleasant. It is in Piccadilly, and so is close to both theatres and shops.' She took her notebook from her handbag. 'I have its telephone number here I think ... yes! 3766. There is an instrument in the hotel office. I am sure that you could use it.'

'But we must stay here tonight, Mamma,' Fanny said firmly. 'Mr Bragg is calling to take me to the theatre.'

'Very well. Now, off you go, both of you, and arrange it. I have work to do.'

Bragg went back to Old Jewry, and told the duty sergeant to expect a call from Dawson's widow. Then he took a cab to University College, in Gower Street. Following directions from a uniformed doorman, he found his way to the library. Around him there were great stacks of books reaching to the ceiling; small tables in the aisles and under the windows, where young men sat turning pages and making notes. There was no one obviously in charge. You could pick up a valuable book, and walk out with it; and nobody any the wiser – assuming they were valuable books... He approached a group of tables where several men were reading.

He cleared his throat. 'I am looking for a...'

There was an angry hissing from the students. One of them gestured angrily towards a notice enjoining silence.

'Sorry,' Bragg muttered. He sat down next to one of the young men. 'I am looking for one of Professor Dawson's students,' he whispered. 'Name of Waller.'

There was a tinge of contempt in the man's smile. 'What is Dawson a professor of?' he asked.

'I wouldn't know his title, but he is an expert in bugs that affect beer.'

'Really! How very utilitarian! This is the classics room. You will have to go to the science stacks ... through that archway there.'

Bragg fought down the desire to clip him round the ear, and followed his directions. He found himself in an identical room, with what seemed like identical students – perhaps a little more intent, a little less well groomed. This time his enquiries elicited responses that were more helpful. He found Waller sitting in a corner, writing intently on a note-pad.

'City police,' he whispered. 'I'd like a word with you.'

'What about?'

'Is there somewhere we can talk properly?'

Waller nodded, and beckoned Bragg to follow him. He stopped under a window in the corridor. 'What is it you want of me?' he asked. He was about twenty-six, Bragg decided, and without the God-given assurance of the upper-class.

'You are one of Professor Dawson's students?' Bragg said.

'Hardly a student. I have taken my first degree, and I am now working towards becoming a Master of Science.'

Bragg raised his eyebrows. 'And you so young!'

'Not exceptionally so ... er ... officer.'

'Sergeant Bragg. I am investigating the death of Professor Dawson.'

34

A look of incredulity crossed his face. 'Our Professor Dawson?'

'Yes. He got himself drowned in a vat at Tyrrell's brewery. I am told you will have an idea of what he was about.'

Waller frowned. 'In general terms, that is true. Professor Dawson has been acting as my supervisor. But we are not researching in the same field, so I cannot give you a detailed account of what he was doing.'

'I doubt I would understand it, if you did. But Lubbock, the chief brewer, said Dawson was looking into something he called wort-spoilers.'

'That is true. He is an authority on coliform bacteria; micro-organisms that act on the sugars in malted barley.'

'What do you mean, "act on"?'

'In technical terms, they reduce the nitrate in the wort to nitrite.'

'That's bad, is it?'

Waller allowed himself a superior smile. 'In the process they produce nitrogen and dimethyl-sulphide gas. There is a powerful smell of cooked cabbage. That particular brew is spoiled.'

'What? Four thousand gallons at a time?'

'Yes.'

'Hmm ... I can see why Tyrrell's let him play around in their little vat. But what about you?'

'My field is wild yeasts.'

'Wild ones?'

'Yes. Brewers yeasts all belong to one family called *Saccharomyces cerevisiae*. But not every member of that family produces good beer.'

'There are some black sheep, are there?'

'Indeed. My interest lies in identifying those yeasts.'

'But yeasts are not bugs.'

'No, they are plants.'

'This is making my head spin!' Bragg complained. 'If you and Dawson were not working on the same subject, how could he be supervising you?'

Waller smiled. 'It is somewhat confusing, I know. But the process of research combines some elements, some disciplines which are common whatever the subject. From time to time I would go to his house, and discuss various matters.'

'He gave you advice? What on?'

'Oh, maintaining rigorous objectivity; an avoidance of a priori reasoning... His experience and acuity have twice saved me from going up a blind alley.'

'Hmm... And what did he get out of this supervision?'

'His reputation was enhanced by every acolyte whose research secured recognition.'

'And what happens to you now?'

Waller frowned. 'It is most unfortunate. I shall have to plough a lonely furrow ... I could find myself schoolmastering after all.'

'I see... Could you explain what Dawson would do, when he went to the brewery?'

'Yes, of course. He was concerned to get samples of the bacteria in the vat, so that he could examine them under a microscope.'

'And you have assisted him in this?'

'I have watched him at work.'

'What did he do, then?'

'He would have several glass bottles. He'd take samples from different parts of the surface of the vat during fermentation, label them and take them back to his laboratory.'

'So he would be up at the top of one of those ladders, leaning over to fill his little bottles?'

'Yes.'

'One can see how it happened... Yes. Well, thank you for your help, Mr Waller. I hope it doesn't affect you too badly.'

Bragg took a cab back to Bedford Square, and rang the bell of Dawson's house. It was eventually answered by a slim, brown-haired woman in her late thirties. A good-looker too.

'Mrs Dawson?'

Her smile was expansive, assured. 'Yes.'

'Sergeant Bragg, of the City of London police. I called earlier, and gave your maid a message that you should ring our Old Jewry headquarters on the telephone.'

She frowned. 'Oh dear,' she said. 'I am afraid that Mildred is at liberty from tea-time on a Saturday; and I have been shopping. I did not receive your message, sergeant.'

'Then, can we go inside?'

She turned and led the way into the

comfortable sitting-room overlooking the square. She seated herself elegantly on a sofa. 'Now, sergeant,' she said with a smile, 'in what way is the City of London police force concerned with me?'

Bragg cleared his throat. This was the worst part of policing, he thought. There was no way you could soften the blow.

'Your husband has had an accident,' he said baldly. 'He was over in the City, at Tyrrell's brewery, taking samples. He seems to have slipped into the vat ... I am sorry to have to tell you that he is dead.'

Bragg watched her face ... a look of puzzlement, bewilderment almost. Was this upper-class stoicism? From his experience he had expected screaming, wailing, fainting even. She leaned back on the sofa and let out a long sigh.

'Oh dear! What a dreadful thing to happen! When was this?' she asked.

'He was found at three o'clock.'

'Where is he?'

'He has been taken to the mortuary, ma'am. I am afraid that there will have to be a post-mortem.'

She gave a grimace. 'Is that really necessary?' she asked.

'The City coroner insists on one, in every case of unexpected death. If I were you, ma'am, I would get in touch with a firm of funeral directors. They will know what to do.'

'Thank you, sergeant,' she said in a low voice. 'I will follow your advice.'

'I will come, in a day or two, to see how you are getting on.'

'Yes ... yes.' Her eyes were fixed on her clenched hands: she was biting her lip to keep back the tears.

Bragg tiptoed out to the street. It was a good thing that he was taking Fanny to the theatre, he thought. At least that would brighten up a depressing day.

2

'You have no idea what a delight it is to be strolling in Hyde Park, Mr Bragg,' Fanny said happily. 'Everywhere is so green and well groomed. And so much space! So different from the streets! There must be hundreds of people here, enjoying the afternoon sun; yet no jostling. Everyone content to stroll and relax.'

'There is little else to do on a Sunday afternoon, miss. Tomorrow most of them will be dashing about, all right!'

She squeezed his arm. 'And I did so enjoy going to the theatre, last night.'

'I was going to mention that,' Bragg said gruffly. 'It was nothing like what I expected it to be. It wasn't right for a well brought up young woman like you.'

'Nonsense! We live too cosy an existence in the country. It is well to be reminded that others do not share it. In any case, the heroine was able to choose her way of life. She was not at the mercy of events. Most women in the audience would envy her that, at least!'

'I suppose your mother would have had some sympathy for her,' Bragg said. 'Not that she is like the play in the slightest... Not at all! But she was left to cope with life as best she could... Except that she had you.'

Fanny laughed. 'And a thriving business, and a comfortable home!'

'A business she intends to sell,' Bragg said, glad to be on firmer ground.

'It was not an easy decision, I assure you. Mamma is not one to shirk her duty. But she is getting older, and less able to cope with the pressures of commercial life. In the beginning, after my father's death, it was a challenge. And the workers rallied to her cause. After all, he had dropped dead before their very eyes ... In any case, there was no other manufactory in Dorchester. There was, in truth, no other employment for them.'

'Ah, but that sells her short. From what I heard, she is a harder taskmaster than your father was ... or should that be task-mistress?'

Fanny laughed. 'She would accept either, so long as it got the same amount of work from the staff!'

'Then, why is she thinking of selling?'

'She has not discussed the background to her decision with me. But she will be sixty years old in a few months. Perhaps that is a factor. And she has become progressively disenchanted with the brewery in recent years. Most of her trusted workers have retired. She says that the current generation have not the same pride in their work; they cannot be relied on. They work only for the wage packet at the end of the week ... And it is not as if she can see a new generation of the family, growing up to succeed her.'

'You don't fancy it yourself, miss?'

Fanny glanced sideways at him. 'I like the idea that the business should continue in the family, of course. But I do not have my mother's determined nature. And I fear that, in a manufactory, control by persuasion is inconceivable.'

'You have no other relatives that could come in?'

'My only other relatives are two maiden

aunts, living in Chiswick.'

'I see... And how are the negotiations going?'

'It is difficult to say. Tyrrell's head brewer – a man called Lubbock – came down some weeks ago.'

'I met him yesterday,' Bragg remarked. 'He seems to know what he is about. And, at least, he is decisive.'

'How incredible! What a coincidence!'

'Not really, miss. There was an accident at Tyrrell's. A man was drowned in a vat.'

'Oh, dear! Breweries are such dangerous places.'

'And what did Lubbock say to your mother?'

'Nothing of substance. He was playing his cards very close to his chest. Nevertheless, he had no significant criticisms.'

'Good! And I am sure your mother can play that game as well as anyone.'

'Indeed!'

Bragg paused, then: 'If you sold the brewery, would you stay living in Bere Regis?' he asked.

Fanny glanced up at him. 'For my part,'

she said, 'I have no indissoluble ties to the village.'

'But you have never lived anywhere else!'

'Then, perhaps it is time for me to move.'

'What, and leave your mother behind?'

Fanny laughed. 'One thing is certain. My mother has no need of my presence.'

They strolled on in companionable silence for some minutes, then Bragg checked. 'That is the Stanhope Gate we are coming to,' he said. 'Do you see that house in Park Lane? The one with the balcony?'

'Yes ... yes, I do! It looks very grand.'

'That is the Marsdens' house.'

Fanny gave a wry smile. 'I am more than a little sorry that we accepted their invitation to tea,' she said. 'It has been such a delightful afternoon.'

'You will like them, miss. For all that he is rubbing shoulders with lords and ladies every day, Mr Marsden is as ordinary as you and me. And Mrs Marsden ... well, there is no side to her at all!'

As they went up the steps to the house, Catherine opened the front door. She gave Fanny a hug, then led the way to a sittingroom and introduced her parents.

'My mother sends her apologies,' Fanny said. 'She is working on some documents relating to the business.'

'Well, you are in good hands with Sergeant Bragg,' Mrs Marsden said, and received a warning frown from Catherine.

'Now, you were going to show me your engagement ring!' Fanny said. 'I heard from Mr Bragg of the terrible experience you had, when you first went to choose a ring.'

Catherine gave a wry smile. 'If being locked up in a sanatorium as insane measures up to that description, then that is true!... I will go and get it.'

'You will have heard that the wedding is to be postponed,' William Marsden said.

'Yes. It seems a great pity.'

'Dashed if I know what the fuss is about!'

'You know perfectly well!' his wife reproved him. 'And you have no more wish to flout the convention than I do.'

William gave a mischievous grin. 'Perhaps we should flout it. I would immediately become unfashionable. Society matrons would no longer ask me to paint their daughters, to turn their goslings into swans. Then we could retire to the south of France!'

Catherine came back. 'I insisted, from the first, that it should be a working, everyday kind of ring,' she said. 'But James and the jeweller were conspiring to foist on me a diamond the size of a pigeon's egg! Now I have got exactly what I want.' She held out her hand for Fanny's inspection. 'You see, it is a little loose. I would hate to pull it off with my glove!'

'A solitaire diamond,' Fanny said admiringly. 'It is beautiful!'

'Come and look at it in the sunlight!' Catherine said excitedly, taking her to the window. 'Look at the colours!'

'Goodness!' Fanny exclaimed. 'Yellow ... red ... even green! Now I know what they mean by brilliant cut!'

'Not that I would treasure it any the less, if it were a tenth of the size,' Catherine said.

There came a jangle of the front door bell, and Catherine rushed to open it herself. Morton's voice could be heard in the hall. They came into the room hand in hand.

Morton crossed to Fanny.

'I am delighted to see you again!' he said. 'I intended to be here an hour ago, but it was not to be.'

'I suppose I ought to congratulate you on your innings yesterday,' William Marsden said wryly. 'Would that it had been against any county, other than Middlesex!'

'I had more than my fair share of luck,' Morton said with a grin. 'Richardson must be one of the best bowlers in the country, at the moment.'

'Did you go down to Ashworth?' Catherine asked.

'Yes.' Morton turned to Fanny. 'Although the death of my brother was expected – and merciful – it has still hit my parents hard. I give them all the support I can.'

Bragg broke in. 'We had an interesting case crop up yesterday,' he said gruffly. 'A drowning.'

'Oh?' Morton said. 'Why is that particularly interesting?'

'It's not often we get anybody drowned in a vat of beer! And there is a coincidence. Hildred's brewery, in Dorset, might be bought up by that very same concern.'

Morton frowned. 'We only have two breweries in the City; Tyrrell's and Whitbread's.'

'Tyrrell's it is!'

'I could get a report into Wednesday's City Press!' Catherine said excitedly. 'What happened?'

'Nothing exciting. The dead man was a professor – a scientist of some sort. It looked as if he had fallen into the vat while taking samples.'

'A professor at University College?' Catherine asked.

'That's right. A man called Dawson. An expert on bugs, I gather. Lived in Bedford Square.'

'Indeed? A well-to-do professor, then.'

'It is strange that it should be at Tyrrell's, is it not?' Fanny said lightly. 'I must say that I distrust coincidences.'

Next morning Bragg got to Old Jewry early. He nodded to the desk sergeant. 'Thanks for giving me the brewery job,' he said. 'Just the ticket!'

'In that case, I'll put your name down against it. Though whether Inspector Cotton will be happy, I don't know.'

'Come on! It's always been finders keepers. Anyway, more than likely it was an accident. Is the Commissioner in?'

'Are you thinking that, if you wheedle Sir William into getting involved in it with you, Inspector Cotton won't be able to take it off you?' the sergeant asked.

Bragg grinned. 'Something like that,' he said.

'Then, there ought to be a drink in it for me!'

'Hasn't there always been?'

Bragg went down the corridor, tapped on the Commissioner's door and went in.

Lieutenant-Colonel Sir William Sumner waved Bragg to a chair, and continued to read a typewritten memorandum. With his balding head and pointed beard, he looked like an ageing Prince of Wales. Eventually he sighed, threw the report into an out-tray and swivelled round in his chair.

'You know, Bragg,' he said plaintively, 'sometimes I positively look forward to my

50

retirement! The way that the Home Office meddles in how police forces are run, seems to be intensifying month by month. When I was persuaded to take this post, it was held out to me that I would be in sole and independent command. Yet I am constantly bombarded with exhortations and memoranda. I tell you, I would happily change places with the lowliest member of the force. Then I would know that what I was doing mattered.'

'It matters to us, sir,' Bragg said earnestly. 'I've heard Metropolitan policemen say they wished they had you as their Commissioner.'

Sir William's eyes widened. 'You have heard that, Bragg?'

'Oh, yes, sir. Too rigid, the Met. Stifles initiative, sir.'

'But initiative, on occasion, can become licence. One must have discipline.'

'Yes, sir... They reckon you have it just right.'

'Well, I hope so... But it would be more rewarding if one's days were not wholly taken up with paper-work. When I was with my regiment, in India, there was always something positive afoot... Here I spend my time arguing for more money from the Corporation; trying to head off complaints from influential businessmen, who believe that their concerns should have priority over all others... One can pay too high a price, Bragg!'

'Well, as it happens, sir, I have an interesting little case you might want to become involved in.'

Sir William's face clouded. 'Yes... Chief Inspector Forbes has been making representations about that. He feels that our arrangement could undermine the authority of Inspector Cotton.'

'But how can that be?' Bragg said unctuously. 'You are the top nob. Inspector Cotton, and all of us, are responsible to you.'

'Yes ... and I will not be made a cipher, Bragg! I did not accept this post to be nothing more than a figurehead.'

'No, sir. Anyway, I don't see this case coming to much. If there are complications, they are on the social side. You are better

52

placed than anyone else in the force, to handle the influential people of the City.'

'Influential people?' the Commissioner echoed warily.

'Yes, sir. I doubt if any crime has been committed at all. But Tyrrell's brewery is involved, and a professor at University College.'

'Tyrrell's brewery?'

'Yes, sir. I was called in on Saturday, when Tyrrell's sent a message that they had found a body in one of the vats.'

'At the brewery?'

'Yes, sir. When I got there they had fished the man out. It seems he was a professor of some sort of science, and Tyrrell's let him experiment at their Tudor Street premises.'

'And are you saying that he died as a result of some criminal activity, Bragg?'

'To be honest, sir, I doubt it. But with Tyrrell's being so influential, and the dead man so eminent, the case has to be handled with care. I doubt if anyone in the force has a wide enough experience of the class of people involved – anyone but you, I mean.'

Sir William smiled. 'Well, of course, I am

here to advise ... yes. Part of my function. And no one could complain of my becoming involved in a mere accident... In any case, my connections could well ease your path.'

'Then, I will report to you for instructions, sir?'

'Yes, Bragg. And I will consult Lady Sumner as to the Tyrrell people. She has her ear much closer to the ground in these matters.'

'Very good, sir. My mind is easier now.'

Bragg got back to his room to find Morton gazing out of the window.

'You have come in, then,' he said gruffly.

'Of course, sir! I thought it worthwhile to call in at the Registrar of Companies office. I looked up Tyrrell's returns.'

'Well?'

'The name of the company is Thomas Tyrrell Ltd. George Tyrrell is the chairman and a substantial shareholder. Other directors have more nominal shareholdings. The names Buller and Hudson have no significance to me, but they could be family. There are also shares held by non-directors.

Some of them are quite substantial holdings. The board could by no means be sure of having its way, if the non-director shareholders voted against a proposition.'

'Hmm... When I was there, on Saturday, they had called in the chief brewer – a chap called Lubbock.'

'He is a director, but apparently holds no shares.'

'Right.' Bragg laughed. 'I put it to him that he should drain the vat, because the corpse could have voided urine in it. He soon let me know money is king!'

'How much beer did the vat hold?'

'Lubbock spoke of two thousand gallons of finished beer – whatever that means.'

'No wonder they did not want to waste it!'

'Yes... But it shows you what matters to them – profit. Why don't we wander over there, and poke about a bit?'

They strolled through the crowded streets. It was already hot. Morton wished that he had put on his lightweight coat; though Bragg was still wearing winter serge!

Bragg paused and knocked his pipe out against the heel of his boot. 'Some funny things happen in this world, lad,' he said pensively. 'I took Miss Hildred to the theatre on Saturday night. A play called *The Notorious Mrs Ebbsmith,* at the Garrick.'

'I saw it when it first opened! Perhaps not the best of choices to take a delicately brought up lady to.'

'No – though Mrs E. got her come-uppance in the end. Anyway, a woman was fished out of the Thames on Sunday, apparently. Her name was Mrs Ebbsmith. Moreover, in her pocket were two tickets for Saturday night's performance at the Garrick.'

'Truth mimicking fiction?' Morton said lightly.

'Not only that. She must have been in the theatre when we were... It makes you think, doesn't it?'

They walked on in silence until they reached the gates of Tyrrell's brewery. Bragg grabbed the arm of a passing workman.

'Can you tell me where the big boss will be?' he asked amiably.

'What, Mr George?'

'George Tyrrell, yes. We have come about

the drowning on Saturday – City police.'

The man led them to the bottom of the yard, and up to an office on the first floor. Bragg knocked and they went in.

'What do you want?' He was grey-haired and stockily built; his shaven cheeks revealed a florid complexion.

'Are you George Tyrrell?' Bragg asked.

'I am.'

'City police. We have come about the death of Professor Dawson, on Saturday ... Sergeant Bragg and Constable Morton.'

'He has been taken to the mortuary. He is not here.'

'I realise that, sir ... I want to get clearer in my mind what he was doing in the brewery.'

'Scientific research. Bugs apparently. If you want details you had better talk to Lubbock, our chief brewer. My side is the sales.'

'But I am sure that you know more about the business than anyone. We would value your assistance.'

Tyrrell seemed about to demur, then he shrugged. 'Fire away, then. But I have a meeting in half an hour.'

Bragg drew up a chair and faced him. 'From the look of the buildings, you have been here a good long time,' he said equably.

'The oldest part of the present buildings goes back to 1730 – though Tyrrell's had been brewing here for a hundred years before that.'

'Things have changed, then.'

'Indeed they have! There was no embankment, no sewerage system, the water for brewing was pumped straight from the river. I tell you, they were hardy people in those days!... Now we use water from the mains supply – though there are those who would tell you the brew is nothing like as good!'

'It's strange to find a brewery so close to the centre of things,' Bragg said.

'That is because you have no sense of history. People look back and see only the castles and palaces. They give no thought to what existed to maintain them. Our brewery has been just as important, in its own way, as the lawyers' chambers in the Temple, next door. If they don't like the smell of brewing, when the wind is from the east, they should up sticks and move themselves.'

'Not comfortable neighbours, then?'

'My solicitors tell me I should be grateful that lawyers have a profound distrust of the law! For my part, I wish they would take us to court; clear it up once and for all. Twenty years, that is all it took to establish our rights. And we have been here a hundred and sixty!'

'They have not got a leg to stand on, then.'

'It does not stop them complaining... Anyway, what do you want from me?'

'I am told that you are the chairman of the company, sir.'

'Yes.' His face clouded. 'I am the last of the Tyrrells.'

'But not the last of the family, surely?'

'No ... I did have a son. But he died five years ago. Just as I was planning to hand over the running of the brewery to him. A bad heart, they said... If you ask me, they didn't know what killed him. But dead he was, and I have had to carry on.'

'You had daughters, then?'

'Yes. Julia and Evelyn. Julia is married to

Tom Bullen, who manages the office here. But a son-in-law is not the same ... and, anyway, they only have a little girl.'

'No grandsons, then?'

'Evelyn has a son – Edward Hudson. Sturdy little chap. But he is only eight. I doubt if I shall be around when he is old enough to be involved.'

'But the word is, you are interested in buying up Hildred's Dorchester brewery.'

Tyrrell looked up sharply. 'Where did you get that from?' he asked. 'Nobody is supposed to know!'

Bragg smiled. 'We are the City police, sir. And you know how rumours rattle around the City.'

'Huh! Well, I don't want anything I say to you rattling round the City!'

'You can be assured of that, sir.'

Tyrrell sighed. 'In any case, the money-men have got us sized up. We are too big to survive by just producing specialist beers. But we are too small to carve out a dominant position in the bulk trade. I have the option of selling the business as it is – take the money and run. Or else we can expand, increase the territorial spread of the company by acquiring other breweries, and go for a public share flotation.'

'And Hildred's would fit in with that?'

'At the right price, it would. It's a fine little brewery, with a good spread of customers in the area around. We could build on that.'

'Right... Now, we gather that Professor Dawson was attached to University College.'

'Yes. I want you to know that he was not working for the company. We just allowed him to experiment here.'

Bragg smiled. 'You did more than that, surely? I understood that you only kept the small vat, in the old vat house, going so that he could do his experiments there.'

Tyrrell shifted uncomfortably in his chair. 'That is true enough,' he said. 'You know, of course, that Whitbread's are our biggest rivals. Now, some years ago, they let a Frenchman come and do some research at their brewery. He was interested in bugs too; and he made some important discoveries. I will not try to explain them; they are beyond me, never mind you! But

Whitbread's name got known wherever beer is brewed. I thought maybe Dawson would do the same for us.'

'So, as far as you are concerned, you will lose by his death.'

Tyrrell sniffed. 'What you haven't had you can hardly lose,' he said.

'No... Who would be aware of the details of Dawson's work?'

'Here, you mean? Fred Lubbock, if anyone. He is my head brewer. If he isn't, I shall want to know why.'

They followed Tyrrell down the stairs, across the yard and into the great vat house. Lubbock was supervising a gang of men, who were skimming yeast from one of the vats. Tyrrell beckoned him over.

'These policemen are back; concerning Professor Dawson's death,' he said. 'Give them any help you can. The sooner they are satisfied, the sooner they will leave us alone.' He nodded at Bragg and hurried away.

'What is it you want?' Lubbock asked irritably. He was thickset, with grizzled hair. His clothes were shapeless and soiled.

'I have brought Constable Morton with

62

me,' Bragg said amiably. 'He's a clever chap; a Master of Arts from Cambridge University. Which means he can count to more than ten. His brain might just about be able to understand what goes on here.'

'You don't need degrees, you need experience!'

'Yes. Well, we will rely on you for that... Now, it seems that Dawson's body was discovered by a man called Jack Thompson. He told Dick White, the foreman, who decided to get Dawson out in case he was still alive.'

'Right.'

'When he was found to be dead, White sent for us.'

'Totally unnecessary,' Lubbock said. 'Anybody could see what had happened.'

'Maybe. But I would like to have a word with Thompson – and White too, if possible.'

'What for?'

'I want to get a picture of the small vat house, as it was when they found Dawson.'

'I am not having you wasting my men's time for nothing!' Lubbock said angrily. 'It was a bloody accident, man! We have better things to do than play games!'

Bragg seized his arm. 'I will have you in a police cell for obstruction, if you don't do as I ask!' he growled. 'Seven days would do you a world of good... Though I doubt if you would be able to boss the men around the same, after that.'

Lubbock went white. 'I am only trying to do my job,' he spluttered.

'The first duty of any citizen is to assist the police,' Bragg said. 'I hope you will see it my way.'

'Yes ... yes, I will do what I can.'

'Good.' Bragg released him.

Lubbock turned to the gang of men, who had been watching the altercation, and beckoned to one of them. He came over, his face expressionless.

'Thompson, find Dick White, then take these men to the old vat house. Tell them everything you know.' He turned on his heel and hurried off.

'You've got a way of persuading people,' Thompson said drily. 'Go through the doorway there. I won't be long.'

Bragg led the way into the old vat house. 'It is just as it was when I came on Saturday,' he said. 'Except that Dawson's body was on a stretcher by the smaller vat.'

'Was it two thousand gallons of beer, that Lubbock mentioned?' Morton asked.

'Finished beer, he said. Whatever that means.'

'I suppose one can see their point – about not wasting it.'

'I was just promising myself that I would try Tyrrell's beer again. It will have to be tonight or never!'

'One thing surprises me,' Morton said. 'The sides of these vats are straight – perpendicular. I had expected them to be curved, like a barrel.'

'Barrels are shaped like that, so they can be handled,' Bragg said. 'Your education has been neglected, lad. Have you never seen them being unloaded at a pub? They slide them down a chute to the ground, then roll them along. Only an inch or two, in the centre, is touching the ground. You can steer it with just a tap of your boot.'

Dick White came in with Thompson. 'It

was Jack, here, that saw him,' he said.

'Right, Mr White,' Bragg said. 'What I am trying to do is get a picture of where everything was when you came in... I gather that the bigger vat, on the left, had nothing to do with the professor's experiments. Is that correct?'

White swallowed nervously. 'I have never seen him messing about in that one,' he said.

'Right. Now, you, Mr Thompson, were the first to find him. For what reason did you come into this vat house?'

'How do you mean?'

'Well, it's a dead end. You cannot get anywhere through it. So you must have been coming for something that was here already.'

A shifty look spread over Thompson's face. He glanced nervously at White. 'I came in for a quick fag,' he said.

'You what?' White exclaimed angrily. 'You know damn well you would be for the sack if you were caught!'

Thompson shrugged. 'Well, I wasn't, was I,' he said.

'What did you see, when you came in?' Bragg asked.

'I dunno ... let me think ... Them ladders. The short one was propped up at the small vat.'

'Put it where it was, will you?'

Thompson took the ladder and placed it at the front of the vat. It rested at a comfortable angle, the top rung level with the edge of the vat. Bragg tested it. It was stable enough. A man could work at the top of it without fear of its sliding from under him.

'Right,' he said. 'And where was the long ladder?'

'Well, it was sort of leaning against the big vat. Not placed proper, if you understand me.'

'Set it as it was.'

Thompson placed the foot of the ladder near the bottom of the small vat then twisted it round so that the top slid along the wall and came to rest against the large vat. Only one upright of the ladder was in contact with the floor. Sideways force, obviously, Bragg thought. Perhaps the professor had leaned too far over, the ladder shifted and in he went.

'Thank you, Mr White. That has been very helpful. I can see how it might have happened ... Tell me, was there anything else unusual that Saturday afternoon?'

White hesitated. 'Not unusual exactly ... I have asked around, of course. I am told there was a young woman seen hereabouts.'

'What time?'

'Early afternoon, I gather. Not that I would set any store by that. Brewery workers are a randy lot, and well paid. And there are plenty of comfortable corners in the stables and stores.'

3

After lunch Bragg and Morton wandered down to the Temple. Although the buildings of Tyrrell's brewery were visible from Temple Gardens, the warehouses of Grand Junction Wharf were right up against its boundary. And they were an eyesore, if anything was, Bragg thought. But they did not smell over-much. Within the Temple itself everything would be orderly and serene – until the wind shifted to the east!

They climbed the stairs to the chambers of the City coroner, Sir Rufus Stone QC. The clerk was sitting at a desk, apparently compiling fee-notes.

'That's right,' Bragg said cheerfully. 'Keep the money rolling in!'

The clerk sniffed. 'People seem more and more reluctant to meet their obligations nowadays,' he complained. 'And when it spreads to the solicitors' profession, one begins to fear for the health of the nation!'

'Get away with you!' Bragg said. 'They just have a better idea than most, of how easily barristers earn their fees! ... Anyway, how likely am I to see him with his coroner's hat on?'

'Marginally more likely than in any other guise. He has seemed rather skittish this morning. But then, he has received an invitation to a garden party at Buckingham Palace!'

'Huh! Buns and tea with a lot of clothes dummies, and maybe catch a glimpse of the old dear from a hundred yards away.'

'Queen Victoria is anything but an old dear, if general report is true,' the clerk said reprovingly, then turned back to his bills.

Morton strolled over to the window and looked down into Pump Court. Many of his Cambridge contemporaries had aspired to become barristers. It had its attractions as a career; jousting in court with an opponent as detached from the realities of the dispute as you were yourself. Doing your best, of course. Winning a famous victory on occasion; having the satisfaction of being part of the best legal system in the world...

And yet it was no more than that – a system dispensing justice. Would Dawson's widow feel she had had justice? Nobody stood up for accident victims and their dependants. When there was no crime, the authorities shrugged their shoulders. Everyone had to die sometime. Many people died in their thirties and forties – always had done. Fewer now than in the old days. Deaths by natural causes, deaths by accident; these were part of the human condition. To be borne stoically. The church's concern, not the state's. An opportunity for charity, to salve the consciences of the wealthy and protected. Not that Dawson's widow would need financial support, if Bragg's description of their residence was anything to go by. But she would be desolated, her life shattered. Bragg had not said if there were children ... Morton caught sight of a tall figure with a mane of grey hair, striding imperiously across the court below.

'Our wait is at an end,' he said. 'Our audience is, I trust, imminent.'

Moments later the door was flung open, and Sir Rufus marched down the corridor to his room. He ignored the policemen

71

totally, banging the door after him.

'Sounds as if he has had a bad morning,' Bragg remarked.

The clerk shrugged. 'One thing I will say for Sir Rufus,' he remarked, 'he can put a reverse behind him. But I would not twist his tail this afternoon if I were you! Give him five minutes, then go in.'

When Bragg and Morton entered, Sir Rufus was tying up a bundle of documents with red tape.

'There are times, Bragg, when I regret forsaking medicine for the law,' he said irritably. 'At least a doctor can make his own judgement, and act on it. In court, your arguments – however cogent – are of no avail, if the judge is determined that his own blinkered view of the facts must prevail!'

'Yes, sir... Though I expect you will be a judge yourself, before long,' Bragg said straight-faced.

Sir Rufus grasped the lapels of his coat and flung back his leonine head. 'I?... Never!' he declaimed.

'I heard a rumour that you are marked out for greater things,' Bragg said earnestly, 'Lord Chancellor, I shouldn't wonder.'

72

'Huh! The world will have gone mad before anything so preposterous occurs! But, my present business with you is no doubt as coroner for the City of London.'

'Yes, sir ... I hardly like to call it a suspicious death; but it was untimely, that's for sure.'

'Facts, man!' Sir Rufus exclaimed. 'Give me the facts.'

'It was an incident at Tyrrell's brewery, on Saturday.'

'Saturday? But it is now Monday – and Monday afternoon, moreover!'

'Yes, sir... It seems that one of the professors at University College had been allowed to carry out some experiments at Tyrrell's brewery. They even operated a special small vat, so that he could use it for his work.'

'What work was that, Bragg?'

'Research into bugs that spoil beer.'

'Very well. And do I take it that he has been done to death?'

'Well, he is dead, no doubt. Though whether he was done to it, I can't say yet. He was fished out of the vat on Saturday afternoon.'

'Hah! And has Burney given you a time of death?'

'We have not seen the pathologist yet, sir. But the beer he was drowned in was fairly warm, so the body would not cool at the usual rate.'

'I see... Drowned in a vat of beer!' He turned to Morton. 'Who was it that drowned in a butt of malmsey?' he asked.

'It is probably apocryphal, sir,' Morton said. 'If you remember, in Shakespeare's *King Richard the Third* there is a skirmish on stage, in which the Duke of Clarence is stabbed – as I recall it, several times. Then, as he is hauled off into the wings, the murderer intimates that, if the stabbing will not suffice, he will drown Clarence "in the malmsey-butt within".'

'I don't see what that has to do with anything,' Bragg said irritably.

'I would hardly expect you to see, Bragg,' Sir Rufus said disdainfully. 'But if we were all to come down to your lowest common denominator of culture, the world would be a poor place indeed!'

Bragg snorted and said nothing.

'Is there any reason to suppose that his

death was anything other than accidental?' Sir Rufus asked.

'We shall have to wait to see what the pathologist finds. But I doubt if it was suicide – that would take drinking yourself to death a bit far!'

'I deplore your unseemly levity, Bragg,' Sir Rufus said sternly. 'Moreover, it is not beyond peradventure that a man might bring an end to his own life in that way.' He took out his diary. 'I will hold a formal inquest, with a jury, on ... let me see ... Friday the twenty-eighth of June. That is in four days' time.'

'Isn't that a bit hasty, sir?' Bragg asked.

'Ample time! We cannot be seen to be dragging our feet in this matter. Tyrrell's are one of the most important trading concerns in the City... Why, I drink their beer myself!'

'Well, don't order anything from them for a week or so,' Bragg said. 'They were loath to waste the beer in the vat. And you know what happens to dead bodies...'

Morton opened the door of Professor Dawson's room in University College. Under the window was a table, littered with open books and papers. It was as if he had jumped up, pushed back his chair and rushed out ... to meet his maker. On either side of the fireplace were bookshelves. In the middle of the floor, under a gasolier, was a desk. More papers were stacked on it. It was a wonder that the man could ever find what he needed. Morton opened the drawers one by one. Pencils, pots of coloured inks, pens. Manuscripts of what seemed to be scientific papers – or drafts of them. In Dawson's writing, anyway. In the top righthand drawer was a litter of loose papers, a few of them in typewriting. Mostly departmental notices. And beneath them ... a diary. Not a substantial business diary, but an elegant pocket diary. The kind of thing one had in one's dress coat, to jot down unexpected invitations at a ball. He opened it. The entries were indeed mere jottings. Initials and times only... Well, if the initials represented people well known to Dawson, the place of the meeting could well be superfluous. He turned the pages, the same pattern was maintained throughout. Not regular but the same two sets of initials: C.E. and J.C. There was even an entry for

J.C. on the twenty-sixth of June – in two days' time. An appointment Dawson was destined not to keep. Morton turned the pages. Nothing for the rest of the year. Strange. A social diary only – restricted to appointments with two people. Kept at the college, not at home. He flipped through the diary to the end. Inside the back cover was a pocket. A piece of flimsy paper protruded from it... It was a florist's bill for the month of May. And sent to Dawson at the college. On two occasions flowers had been delivered 'as per your instructions'. Interestingly enough, the address of the florist was nowhere near Dawson's residence. Melton Street! That was near Euston station. An easy walk from University College, but not an area Mrs Dawson was likely to frequent. Morton put the bill back into the diary, and slipped it into his pocket.

The cab set Bragg down in front of the Dawsons' house. He noted with approval the drawn curtains, the great bow of black crape tied to the knocker. The door was opened by the young maid. She was dressed in black, and a black lace cap was perched on her head. That seemed to be going a bit far, Bragg thought; though the Queen had gone overboard with her mourning, after Prince Albert died. The maid showed him solemnly into the sitting-room. In what light crept through the curtains, he could see that the desk had been pushed to a wall. A settee was in front of the fireplace now, and an unseasonal fire flickered in the grate. Well, a fire always gave you comfort. And Mrs Dawson would need all the comfort and support she could get.

She rose from a chair as he entered, her face drawn. She was wearing a black woollen dress with a full skirt, that accentuated the slimness of her waist. Her bodice was covered in black crape; at the neck was a narrow band of jet bead embroidery. For an unexpected death, she had managed to fit herself out in the highest fashion, Bragg thought uncharitably. Marshall & Snelgrove probably. She would want to look her best, whatever the occasion.

'Are you bearing up all right?' he asked sympathetically.

'I have not been to ... to see him,' she said in a flat voice. 'I do not even know where he is!'

'Still at the mortuary, ma'am. You have engaged a firm of undertakers?'

She shivered. 'Yes... Thank you for the considerate way you carried out your duty, officer.'

'That's all right, ma'am. I have spoken to the coroner. There is to be an inquest on the twenty-eighth. A full-dress affair, with a jury. I expect you would want your solicitor to be there.'

'Is an inquest really necessary, officer? It will only serve to prolong the pain of loss.'

'Well, it was an unexpected death, and the City coroner is not one to cut corners. In a way, it's a kind of compliment. Shows your husband was well thought of.'

'I ... I wish I could know that he did not suffer,' she said, dabbing at her eyes with a black-edged handkerchief.

'They say that drowning is a peaceful sort of death, ma'am.'

'I cannot believe that ... I cannot understand anything! Edward could swim like a fish!'

'Did your husband have any enemies?' Bragg asked quietly.

Her eyes widened. 'You do not believe that it was an accident!' she cried accusingly.

'You will understand, ma'am, that we must cover all possibilities in our report.'

She shivered. 'He was so gregarious and amiable; I cannot believe that he had enemies. Rivals, perhaps, but nothing that could lead to ... to this!'

'What about these rivals, then?'

'I do not wish to make too much of this, sergeant. All successful men have rivals. It is the way society thrives and renews itself. But...'

'But what, ma'am?'

'There is a colleague of my husband at the college. His name is Dr Hunt – Albert Hunt, I believe. He is a senior lecturer in the science faculty. I believe he is a few years older than my husband. From what Edward said at the time, they were rivals for the vacant professorial chair that my husband was selected to fill.'

'So Hunt must be clever and ambitious?'

'I suppose so. I am afraid I have had but little contact with him. He is an intense, somewhat morose man; and a bachelor. We have only met at college functions.'

Bragg took a cab to Golden Lane, and went into the City mortuary. Noakes, the pathologist's assistant, was hosing down one of the grey marble slabs that were ranged along the walls.

'Is his eminence in?' he asked.

'Doing yours now,' Noakes said in a matter-of-fact tone. 'Go in, if you like.'

Bragg went to the far end of the mortuary, and into the examination room. The portly figure of Dr Burney was stooped over the gaping abdominal cavity of a male corpse. His mouth sagged open in a cherubic smile.

'Being a bit particular, aren't you, sir?' Bragg said in a bantering tone. 'I am damn sure he didn't drink himself to death!'

Burney peered at him over half-moon glasses. 'Ah, sergeant... Where is your acolyte today?' he asked.

'Morton has had so much time off, playing cricket, he's got to do a bit on his own!'

'Hmm. Still, many people would approve – not least the City police service. How many forces have an international cricketer in their ranks?'

'I thought you were too dedicated to bother about things like that,' Bragg said sourly.

'You would be surprised at how useful it can be, Bragg. To toss off a remark to one's students, that Police Constable Jim Morton called in on a case, can confer a most extraordinary cachet on one.'

'So you want me to go away, and come back when he is free to come too?'

'Not at all, sergeant. In matters outside the strict limits of science, I am quite prepared to embroider the truth – in a good cause, naturally!'

'Well, how about a bit of unembroidered truth on Professor Dawson here?'

'I can give you all the information that you would consider relevant, I expect.'

'Well, then?'

'There is no doubt that the cause of death was drowning. I examined the fluid in the lungs. It contained yeast cells. Now, before you laud my perspicacity, I should say that Noakes was told he had been fished out of a vat at Tyrrell's brewery. I was testing the fluid by way of confirmation. But, from a forensic point of view, that did not take me very far. The subject is five feet eleven inches tall. How big would you say a vat is?'

Bragg frowned. 'The one he was drowned in would be fourteen feet high and, say, ten feet across.'

'You see, if a man of the subject's height and strength were merely to fall into a ten-foot-wide vessel of liquid, he would be able to flail about enough to reach the side, even if he could not swim.'

'In fact,' Bragg said, 'his feet were sticking over the edge of the vat. It was seeing them that alerted the workmen.'

Burney beamed with satisfaction. 'Excellent!' he cried. 'You have solved my remaining conundrum. Look at the subject's legs. Can you see the abrasions along the shin bone of both legs?'

'It certainly looks as if they had been scraped by something.'

'Indeed. In the normal course it would have been intensely painful. But, what if the subject could not feel the pain? What if he was, in fact, unconscious at that point ... I then examined the obvious areas, and found what I was seeking ... Just lift the right shoulder, will you? Turn him on his side.'

Reluctantly Bragg complied.

'You see the patch where I have shaved away the hair – by the right ear?'

'There is an abrasion – the skin is broken!'

'Yes. The subject received a blow there, shortly before death supervened. Did you find any weapon at the scene?'

'Well, there were some pieces of timber around. One of them floating in the vat where Dawson was working.'

Burney's grin became bashful. 'Then all the pieces fit together. It seems beyond peradventure that another person was present. The sequence of events was probably something like this. Dawson and this assumed person were carrying out some procedure in the vat – presumably standing on ladders. At some point the assailant struck Dawson on the head, with considerable force. Dawson fell unconscious into the vat, with his legs projecting over the side of the vessel. And, in fact, he drowned. His assailant endeavoured to fully conceal the body in the vat, by pushing on the legs. That is when the abrasions were inflicted. One presumes that he became fearful of discovery and, abandoning the attempt, fled.'

'You can read all that into it, can you, sir?' Bragg asked.

'For your ears only, sergeant. My report will merely say that the cause of death was drowning.'

'So the jury might find it was accidental.'

'That would be their privilege, in the absence of evidence.'

'But you think it was murder?'

Burney beamed ghoulishly at him. 'Oh, yes, sergeant. I am sure of it.'

'Can you give me any idea of a time, sir?'

'I understand that considerable heat is applied, at certain stages of the brewing process. What was the temperature of the liquid in which he was found?'

'It was a small vat house; only two vats. And it was uncomfortably warm in there.'

'Yes... Noakes recorded the body temperature of the subject, as soon as it reached the mortuary. In normal circumstances, the temperature of a corpse will drop by roughly one degree an hour. So one can estimate the time of death with reasonable

85

precision. But not in this case, sergeant. I am reluctant to admit that the queen of sciences has failed you. I suggest that you would be better served by finding the last person who saw him alive, and working from there.'

When Bragg got in to Old Jewry next morning, he found that Morton was already there.

'How did you get on yesterday?' he asked.

Morton shrugged. 'I found nothing that was earth-shattering; on the face of it, anyway. I get a feeling that Dawson was something of a philanderer. I found this diary in his desk ... with an interesting bill in the back pocket.'

Bragg examined them carefully. 'Two women plus his wife, eh? Could he keep all three of them happy, I wonder? C.E and J.C. Have we come across anybody at the brewery that would tie in with those initials?'

'Not yet, I think.'

'Mind you, Tyrrell's must have scores of employees.'

'Indeed. But not many, I suspect, whose

wives would be to Dawson's taste.'

Bragg laughed. 'Steady on, lad!' he said. 'Let's keep our feet on the ground!'

Morton shrugged. 'I thought it might be worth going to the florist, to see if we can discover the names behind the initials after all, that bill is unlikely ever to be paid.'

'Right, lad. It's worth a try; particularly as we are now working a murder case.'

'Murder?' Morton echoed in surprise.

'Don't get too excited. It is all circumstantial, as far as I can see. But I have never known Professor Burney wrong – not when he is as definite as he was yesterday.'

'On what grounds does he believe that Dawson was murdered?'

'First of all, he found a fresh laceration on the skull, at the back of the head. He says it was made by a blow that would have knocked him unconscious. As he sees it, Dawson was up a ladder, taking samples from the vat. Some unkind person – who was presumably also up a ladder at the vat – clouted him one with a blunt instrument. Whereupon Dawson fell forward into the vat.'

'Face down, presumably.'

'I take it so... Now, whether our murderer held his head under the surface or not, I don't know. But there were yeast cells in the liquid Burney took from the lungs. So there is no doubt about what killed him.'

'Drowned while unconscious,' Morton murmured.

'Yes. Now, according to Burney, the murderer started to shove the body further into the vat, to hide it. If you remember, there was a metal hoop right round the very top of the vat. When he examined the body, he found both shins had been scraped raw. Then, for some reason, the murderer stopped; and left him with his feet sticking out over the rim.'

'Perhaps he heard someone coming?' Morton suggested.

'Could be... But one thing is for sure. He was no stranger to the brewery. He must have known his way to the old vat house; and he was so familiar there, that the workers didn't even notice.'

'One of the workers might well be the killer,' Morton said.

'Yes... Any one of them would be able to bide his time. And Dawson would think nothing of it if, say, Lubbock had climbed up a ladder beside him, ostensibly to look at the brew.'

'And he would be just as reluctant to be found there, after he had attacked Dawson.'

'Hmm. But why? Granted that any of a score of people could have done it, we are no further forward.'

'I see it as a crime of passion!' Morton said buoyantly. 'Someone had discovered that Dawson was sending flowers to his wife, and decided to end it – permanently. All we have to do, is find an employee whose surname begins with the letter E or C, and arrest him!'

'Stop pissing about, lad!' Bragg said gruffly. 'This is serious. For my money, we don't know enough about the man. We shall end up chasing hares... Who was that other academic, who used to mess about at the brewery before Waller?'

'Turnbury?'

'Yes, that's the one. Where does he hang out?'

'I gather that, having reached the eminence of junior lecturer, he has been given a room of his own at the college.'

89

'Then let us go and have a word with him. Get us a cab, will you?'

They found Turnbury in an attic room at the college. To Morton it seemed scarcely larger than a decent broom closet. But it had his name on the door; witness that he was now a person of some standing, had emerged from the herd. He was approaching thirty, handsome and confident; without doubt attractive to women.

'We are having a chat with everybody who knew Professor Dawson,' Bragg said cheerfully. 'We gather that you were one of his recent students.'

'He was my supervisor, when I was working for my Master's degree,' Turnbury said quietly.

'Like Waller is now?'

'I imagine so.'

'And what are you researching into?'

Turnbury smiled. 'Now that I have been appointed a college lecturer, I have little time for research.'

'I see. Then, what is your line of expertise?'

'Bacteria.'

90

'The same as Professor Dawson. That must have been handy for you. I expect that he gave you the odd tip.'

Turnbury snorted. 'Dawson's main concern was the advancement of his own reputation, not that of others.'

'I see. Selfish, was he?'

'No. I am in danger of giving you a false impression. Scientific research ought to be a collaborative activity. Obviously the continuous pooling of information would accelerate the process of discovery. But the competitive nature of mankind leads even the most objective of scientists to crave the credit for what he has discovered.'

'I see. That apart, what was he like?'

Turnbury frowned. 'Obviously we did not move in the same social circles. He was a genuinely eminent scholar, and treated as such by his peers. He also had the foresight to marry a wealthy wife. This gave him the entree to society with a capital S.'

'In my experience of Society,' Morton said, 'the mere possession of wealth does not take one very far. Personal qualities count for more than money.'

Turnbury looked at him, a touch of

disdain in his smile. 'I am sure that you are right,' he said dismissively.

'This Waller chap,' Bragg said, breaking in. 'He tells us that he is researching into plants. Yet Dawson was his supervisor.'

Turnbury shrugged. 'Scientific rigour is applicable over the whole field of research,' he said.

'So he told us. He seemed to think it was an honour to have Dawson peering over his shoulder.'

Turnbury laughed. 'I would hardly go so far!' he said. 'Yet I would acknowledge that I owe my present post, in some measure, to his influence.'

'But you won't lose it, now he is gone?'

'No. You misunderstand me. I like to think that I was appointed a lecturer purely on my own merits. But the college authorities would expect Dawson to attract able students, and would accept his judgement of a man's ability.'

'Right... Now, you will be able to explain, in simple terms, what it was that Dawson was studying.'

Turnbury smiled indulgently. 'I will try, officer,' he said. 'It has been realised for decades that a brewery is a natural laboratory for research. You have heard of Louis Pasteur?'

'The French chemist?' Morton said.

'Yes. About twenty years ago he spent a period in London, studying beer ferments at Whitbread's brewery. It was he who first identified, through the use of his microscope, the organisms that can spoil beer.'

'And gave rise to a succession of researchers in these natural laboratories.'

'Indeed.'

'Not only into bacteria, but into various yeasts also?'

'Yes. These things are in the air all around us, invisible to the naked eye. At a certain stage in the brewing process, after the wort has been cooled to around sixty degrees, it is susceptible to infection by bacteria and wild yeasts.'

'Infection!' Bragg exclaimed. 'It sounds as if it's alive!'

'The infecting agents certainly are. And they can multiply at an astonishing rate. This is the point in the brewing process where the liquid is poured into a vat for fermentation. One might say that a window is opened to scientists for a few days. Fermentation takes place over a period of five to seven days. But once the yeast begins to grow, the danger of infection diminishes.'

'We are told that infected beer stinks to high heaven,' Bragg remarked.

'Indeed! Brewers would not tolerate the presence of scientists on their premises, if there were not sound commercial benefits to be gained.'

'Yes... Would you mind telling me where you were between, say, two o'clock and four o'clock on Saturday afternoon?'

Turnbury frowned. 'I was in the college library all afternoon, until, I suppose, half-past four.'

'Is there anyone who could vouch for that?'

'Why, yes. I had a long, and somewhat heated discussion with Waller.'

'What about?'

Turnbury gave a superior smile. 'A mercifully rare bug called *Zymomonas*. It can attack beer in the cask. It produces both hydrogen sulphide and acetaldehyde; which adds up to an unbearable stench.'

'But what is there to argue about?'

'Whether it is air-borne, or water-borne, or comes ultimately from the soil... Waller has a habit of using such debates as a way of picking one's brains.'

'Is that not legitimate?'

'To a certain degree, yes. But it is hardly welcome.'

'And is he a bright lad?'

'He must be. Dawson would never have tolerated a dullard.'

'Hmm...' Bragg pondered, then: 'And what will happen now?' he asked.

'In what respect?'

'Well, the college is a professor short.'

Turnbury smiled. 'That post must be filled as soon as possible, I would suppose.'

'And who is in the running?'

'I would have no idea! It could be someone from a different discipline. It could be that an existing professor from a provincial university might be attracted by the superior research facilities here ... I doubt if anyone from Oxford or Cambridge would apply.'

'But you are saying that it would have to be advertised?'

'Well, yes. That is the universal practice. Though often it is no more than a gesture, if there is an obvious candidate.'

'Hmm... And would there be an obvious candidate on the staff here?'

Turnbury pursed his lips. 'I believe that Albert Hunt has ambitions in that direction.'

'Who is he?'

'A senior lecturer in the science faculty. He is a physicist, and an authority on thermodynamics, I believe.'

'Then I don't suppose he was doing research at Tyrrell's as well.'

Turnbury laughed. 'I suppose the brewing process employs thermodynamics, in some measure. But I doubt it!'

Bragg and Morton ate a snack for lunch, in Euston station, then strolled to Melton Street. The florist's shop was quite impressive, with buckets of blooms giving the pavement a festive air. The shop would no doubt thrive on the passing trade, Bragg thought. Guilty husbands buying a sop for their wives, because they had stayed drinking after work... They stood at the back of the shop while the young woman assistant gave precise instructions to a customer as to how he could prolong the life of his flowers. The man was nodding assent at each stricture, but Bragg knew damn well it would be a waste of breath. The gesture was all that would matter to him. Women were naturally inclined towards caring for things. They gave life and they naturally respected it. Not men... Queer things, flowers. Nice in themselves, of course. But they had acquired a kind of power, of mystery. They would put the seal on an erring husband's protestations, however false they were. Or proclaim undying affection from some adulterous chancer... Not in the country, though. There you grew your own flowers. If you gave any away, it was because you had more than enough for your own needs. They weren't a commodity, they had not acquired any symbolic status, they were just ... flowers!

'Can I help you?' The young woman was smiling sweetly at Morton.

'We are City police officers,' Morton said, flourishing his warrant-card. 'I would like you to examine this account.' He passed over the bill he had found in Dawson's diary.

She took it, and glanced at it frowning.

'Well, what about it?' she asked.

'It was sent from this shop?'

'Yes, Mr Dawson. Is there anything wrong with it?'

'No... I mean, I am not Dawson. I want you to give me some information about the account.'

She drew in her breath. 'Ooh! I don't think I can do that! Mr Webster impressed on me, when he took me on. "It's a confidential service," he would say, "Secrets of the confessional!" It would be as much as my job's worth!'

'But a man has been killed!'

She cocked her head on one side. 'Not by me, he hasn't,' she said waspishly. 'And not with our flowers!'

'You misunderstand me,' Morton said patiently. 'The man who received this account, your customer, has been murdered.'

'Not for sending flowers, I know!'

'Perhaps because he sent flowers on these particular occasions.' She frowned. 'It is

98

nothing to do with me!' she said mulishly. 'You will have to talk to Mr Webster.'

'Then, where is he?'

'He's gone home, hasn't he? Up at four o'clock, going to the market! He can't work all afternoon as well!'

As Morton hesitated, Bragg strode over to the shop door and banged it shut. 'There will be no more customers today, until you have told us,' he said angrily.

'Well, it won't be my fault!'

Bragg crossed to her, towering over her. 'You know what you are doing, madam?' he growled. 'You are obstructing the police in the execution of their duty! Have you ever seen the inside of Holloway prison?'

'No,' she said in a small voice.

'You'll be slopping out there for six months, if you carry on as you are!'

'But we don't belong to the City police! We have the Metropolitan police.'

Bragg lifted his arm to shake her, then let it fall to his side. 'You don't belong to the City police!' He began to laugh. 'We are not insurance companies, you know! You haven't got a choice as to which police force you will join!'

'But Mr Webster...' Her voice tailed away.

'All right. We will lock you in the lavatory. That way you can tell Mr Webster you did your best.'

'There is no need for that!'

'Then, show me where the ledger is. I can just about find my way in it.'

'No! I would get told off even worse, if you did that.'

Bragg smiled at her. 'Then, why don't you give the constable what he is asking for? Nobody will ever know.'

'What is it you want?'

'The names and addresses of the women that Dawson was sending flowers to.'

'Will you promise me you won't tell Mr Webster?'

'I promise.'

She gave him a searching glance, then went through a curtain in the rear wall. She was gone for some time. Bragg began to think that she had slipped away down some back alley. People were rattling the street door, peering through the glass. Then she came back, a sheet of paper in her hand. Her writing was childlike; a careful copper-plate.

Mrs Caroline Eldridge,
12, St John's Wood Terrace,
Marylebone.

Mrs Jennifer Calder,
St Mark's Vicarage,
Whitefriars Street,
City of London.

Bragg and Morton took a cab to Tyrrell's brewery. They found Lubbock in his office, writing laboriously in a leather-bound book. He looked up.

'What are you back for?' he asked irritably. 'I reckon the ratepayers ought to know about the money you lot spend, pestering people to no purpose.'

Bragg nodded. 'You could be right, sir. But they would be even more concerned to make sure that we solve a murder in the City.'

Lubbock's head jerked round. 'Murder?' he said. 'What? This one? Dawson?'

'We shall have to wait for the inquest, on Friday. But Professor Burney, the pathologist, reckons it was murder. And I've never known him to be wrong.'

'Oh, bugger!' Lubbock said emphatically. 'The old man will be stark staring mad over this.'

'George Tyrrell?'

'Yes. He has put a lot of time and effort into his plans for the future. It would only take something like this, to spoil it all.'

'You mean the public flotation?'

Lubbock looked thunderstruck. 'How the hell did you get to know?' he asked.

'We are the City police, sir. It's our job to know these things.'

'Bloody hell! I'll look twice before I wipe my arse, when you lot are around.'

'We are only interested in Dawson's death.'

'That sod! I don't know why we encouraged him.'

'Presumably to get on level terms with Whitbread's and their Pasteur,' Morton remarked.

Lubbock frowned. 'Nothing was ever going to come of it!' he said irritably. 'Brewing is an art. If it wasn't, we would have a machine that would do it by now.'

'Can you explain the brewing process

to us – simply?'

He sighed. 'If I must, I suppose... In the very beginning they did not brew beer as we know it, they brewed what we would call ale.'

'As in India Pale Ale?' Bragg asked.

'Yes. That is made from malt, yeast and water. Brewing is a totally natural process – no chemicals whatever.'

'And, at Tyrrell's you will keep it that way?'

'While I am here, anyway... Where was I?'

'Brewing ale.'

'Right. The malt is made from barley grain. We buy ours in, ready malted, from the West Country. What the malters do, is steep the grain till the shoots begin to germinate. This happens in a couple of days. Then this green malt is spread over a heated floor, kept damp, and turned from time to time.'

'Does the seed germinate normally in the air?' Morton asked.

'It has a root as well as a shoot, if that is what you mean... Anyway, the green shoot grows for eight to ten days. At that point it can be described as malt; all the goodness is in the shoot, and the root has withered.

103

They then dry this malt in a kiln, bag it and send it to us as and when we need it.'

'So you can get this dried malt all the year round?'

'Yes. Even in a bad year we can get enough. One of our shareholders is a big barley farmer. It's in his interest, every way, to see us right.'

'No doubt. So what happens next?'

'Are we going to brew ale or beer?' Lubbock asked.

'Beer,' Bragg said firmly. 'We want none of this IPA gnat's piss.'

A trace of a smile touched Lubbock's lips. 'Right,' he said. 'Well, the first thing we do is take the dried malt and crush it. We then have a mixture of roughly ground flour and husks. This is called grist.'

'As in "grist to her mill"?' Morton asked.

'Yes. Then we mix the grist with water at around a hundred and fifty degrees Fahrenheit in a mash tun, to give us a porridgey mixture.'

'Quite warm, then.'

'Warm enough to break down the starch in the barley, and convert it into sugars of various kinds. The men keep stirring the mixture for twelve hours and more, until I judge all the goodness is in the liquid. This wort is filtered out of the bottom, leaving the husks and so on behind.'

'So what happens next?' Bragg asked.

'The wort is boiled in a great copper kettle for a couple of hours, to sterilise and concentrate it. And, since we are making beer, not ale, we start adding the hops! These not only give it the flavour we want, they help the beer to keep longer. And since we filter out the wort through the layer of hops, it helps towards getting a clear brew.'

'But, at this stage there is presumably no alcohol in the liquid,' Morton said.

'Right. And clearly we cannot go pitching live yeast into near-boiling wort. So we have to cool it, in large shallow vessels. As it cools we get a scum forming, which we skim off. Then we keep our fingers crossed.'

'Why is that?'

'As our unfortunate friend Dawson would have told us, this is the stage when the wort is liable to get infected by bacteria and wild yeasts. Not that you will know it for a day or two.'

'He was interested in what went on in the

vats.' Bragg remarked.

'Yes. That is where the fermentation takes place. After cooling, and filtering it again, the wort is pumped into a vat, and our special strain of yeast is pitched in. At this stage the wort is at about sixty degrees, and over the week of fermentation it could go up another ten. Unfortunately these are the very conditions that the wort-spoilers thrive on.'

'Both the bacteria and the wild yeasts?' Bragg asked.

'Both. And either of them can spoil a whole vat of beer. The brewers' yeast we put in will increase up to eight-fold. Wild yeasts and bacteria even faster. There is no certain way of preventing it. All you can do is keep everything as clean as you can, and cross your fingers.'

'Are you saying that you have really got no benefit from having the likes of Dawson and Waller messing about here?' Bragg asked.

'No substantial benefit to date. But you can never tell, can you? And George Tyrrell likes to be seen to support scientific research.'

'I see. It's a good thing Pasteur didn't get

drowned at Whitbread's, isn't it? But I don't suppose anyone had a reason to murder him.'

Lubbock shook his head. 'I still cannot believe it,' he said.

'Tell me,' Bragg said. 'Have you any employees whose surnames begin with E?'

Lubbock frowned. 'How the hell should I know?' he exclaimed. 'You will have to ask at the wages office.'

'It would not be a labourer.'

Lubbock frowned again. 'I cannot think of any.'

'It seems as if I shall have to take you into my confidence... Does the name Eldridge mean anything?'

'Eldridge is the name of a partner in Fortescue & Blount, the solicitors to the company. Lives in St John's Wood.'

'I am told that a woman was seen here on the afternoon of the murder.'

Lubbock's face darkened. 'I know there is chatter about Dawson and Mrs Eldridge. There was talk that Eldridge was going to divorce her. But it was no more than talk... Anyway, I cannot see her seeking him out - here of all places!'

'Has she ever been to the brewery?'

'She comes to the Christmas party.'

'Held here?'

'In the canteen.'

'Was Dawson here as well?'

'Look!' Lubbock said angrily. 'It is not my business to snoop on other people. They are free to do what they like and take the consequences!'

'Yes,' Bragg said grimly. 'That could be exactly what happened.'

Lest Lubbock should let the cat out of the bag, Bragg decided that they should go straightway to St John's Wood. The Eldridges lived in a substantial red-brick villa, with a carriage drive in front. But the gravel bore no imprint of wheels. It would be pointless to keep your own carriage, in this modern age of hackney cabs and trains. Morton tugged at the bell-pull, and a smartly dressed maid appeared.

'Is Mrs Eldridge in, please?' he asked.

The girl looked at them doubtfully. 'She's in all right,' she said. 'But it's a bit late for receiving, isn't it?'

Morton smiled. 'This is not a social call.

Would you please tell her that we are police officers, and that we would like to see her.'

A startled look crossed the maid's face. 'Wait there, then,' she said and closed the door on them.

'That's a bit cheeky,' Bragg said. 'What if madam skips off round the back?'

'I doubt if she could do anything so enterprising,' Morton said. 'The cosseted life of a society lady does not prepare her for acts of derring-do!'

'But how many of them are carrying on with another man on the side?'

'Many a one, I would think.'

The door opened and the maid conducted them down a passage, to a room at the back of the house. It overlooked a lawn, edged with rose bushes. A slim, brown-haired woman of medium height rose to greet them. Her smile was confident, her manner relaxed.

'Mrs Caroline Eldridge?' Morton asked.

'Yes. Please do sit down. This is a new experience for me! Though why you should wish to see me, as distinct from my husband, is a mystery.'

'We understand that you were a friend of

Edward Dawson,' Morton said.

For a moment it was as if she expected him to continue; then she frowned. 'I certainly knew him,' she said.

'And you are clearly aware of his death.'

'My husband informed me of it.'

'We have reason to believe that there was a close relationship between you.'

'Relationship?'

'An *affaire de coeur*.'

'Goodness! A cultured policeman! What next?'

'Also that it continued until he was murdered, last Saturday.'

The colour drained from her face. 'I was told that it was an accident,' she said.

'Who by?'

'John, my husband.'

'When did he tell you this?'

'On Monday. He was apparently consulted professionally, as to the company's legal position.'

'It is quite clear, from Dawson's diary, that you and he were lovers.'

'That was very silly of him,' she said sharply.

'How did you come to meet him?'

She frowned. 'I have been taken, by my husband, to Christmas parties at Tyrrell's brewery for many years now. He apparently thinks that my presence helps to strengthen his professional bond with the company. On such occasions I am enjoined to be sociable and charming towards the principals of the client concern. And it adds a little amusement, to what is generally a thoroughly boring experience... I hate being shown over factories; particularly smelly ones! To begin with, I thought that Edward Dawson was a director of the company. He had such presence; and could talk so interestingly about what went on at the brewery. And then I discovered that he was, in fact, someone much more eminent.'

'When did you meet him?' Morton asked.

'It was at Christmas, three years ago. Yes, we have been ... well, if you must, we have been lovers for over two years.'

'And your husband has been aware of this?'

'Yes,' she said defiantly.

'Did he not try to stop it?'

Her lip curled. 'If he had been able to discharge his duty in that regard,' she said,

111

'the situation might never have arisen. In the event, he was hardly in a position to take action. He would have become an object of derision in the profession.'

'So, are you saying that he became reconciled to your affair with Dawson?'

She gave Morton a coquettish smile. 'You have a very old-fashioned attitude to affairs of the heart, officer,' she said. 'We women are no longer subservient chattels – whatever the law says. And, after all, Rosalie Dawson is carrying on a liaison with Charles Anscombe. As it happens, she met him at a Tyrrell's Christmas party also!'

'We have not met his name before,' Morton said.

'He is a partner in Gosling & Hoare, a bank situated in Fleet Street.'

'And, since he was at the party, can we assume that Gosling & Hoare also act for Tyrrell's?'

Caroline Eldridge shrugged. 'I presume that they must do,' she said.

Bragg crossed to the corner of the sitting-room in the St James's Hotel, and greeted Fanny and her mother.

'Will you have coffee?' Amy asked brusquely.

'No, thank you, ma'am.'

'Then, sit down. I want your views on the Tyrrell people... I had a meeting at the brewery this morning. George Tyrrell was suspiciously charming. But fine words will still butter no parsnips.'

'I would say that he will drive a hard bargain,' Bragg said.

'I expect so. But if it is fair, all well and good... It is Lubbock that intrigues me. It was he who came down to Dorchester, as you know.'

'He must have given the board a favourable report,' Bragg said. 'Tyrrell told me it was a fine little brewery, with a good spread of customers.'

'I'll give him "fine little brewery"! He is not likely to find a bigger one outside the cities. And he would hardly have the money to buy such a one. If he really wants to expand, he could not do better than buy my brewery, at my price!'

'Mamma thinks that George Tyrrell is holding out for a lower figure, just because she is a woman,' Fanny said.

113

'Surely not?' Bragg laughed. 'Then he will find out his mistake.'

'In the end,' Amy said, 'he will listen to the likes of Lubbock, but he will make up his own mind.'

'Which is what you would expect ... Who else was at the meeting?'

'There was only George Tyrrell and a man called Eldridge.'

'The solicitor?'

'Yes... A nothing of a man! Colourless... Only spoke when spoken to. But not placid. Somehow all wound up inside... I would not want him around me.'

There was a pause in the conversation, then: 'I was having some instruction about brewing, this morning, from Lubbock,' Bragg said. 'He was explaining about wort-spoilers.'

'Huh!' Amy exclaimed. 'Very convenient! If anything goes wrong with a brew, blame it on them!'

'So, how do you cope with them?'

'First of all, I leave the responsibility where it belongs with the head brewer. But I do see that everything is cleaned and polished till it shines – and that before every brew, not just once a week... But I would not have built my brewery on the Thames in the first place. Think of all the filth in the air, and on the streets. They say that they use mains water for the actual brewing – and no doubt they do. But for washing down, they pump the water straight from the Thames... Cheaper, of course. But a spoiled brew would soon wipe out what you had saved.'

4

Morton got in to Old Jewry, next morning, to find Bragg deeply engrossed in a newspaper. He looked up.

'I reckon the Liberals are going to be in trouble, lad,' he said. 'What decent government would get itself thrown out of office, just because the army is not up to scratch? It's not as if anyone is rattling their sabres at our gates.'

'According to my father, there are some formidable sabres being sharpened,' Morton said. 'German and Austrian among them. The Liberals deserve to be punished for their complacency.'

'Huh! I might have expected that the son of a general would stick up for the Tories. But no good will come of this election, mark my words!... Anyway, where is Dawson's funeral to be?'

'Manor Park cemetery, sir. We can get a

train from Liverpool Street station.'

'We shall look damn stupid, if Professor Burney has got it wrong – if Dawson did just overbalance and hit his head on the vat.'

'Yet we can hardly discount an opinion which is likely to be the basis of the coroner's findings.'

Bragg pushed back his chair. 'No, lad. Anyway, it will give you the chance to see the grieving widow. Not that she had shed many tears when I saw her.'

'I see from the newspaper, that there is to be a memorial service at St George's church, Bloomsbury, on the second of July. I take it that you would wish to go.'

'We had better. Though it is likely to be an academic showpiece. In the meantime, let us pop in on the other object of Dawson's love-posies.'

The sun was already hot as they strolled through the busy streets. Bragg cast an envious eye at Morton's lightweight lounge jacket. He ought to get one himself, he thought, instead of sweating like a pig in his frock coat. But Morton could afford it... Anyway, if he did splash out and get one, the weather would change the next day. He would never get any wear out of it.

'There is the vicarage,' Morton said. 'I wonder if the vicar himself will be in.'

'He might be. There would hardly be more than a handful of people actually living round here.'

Bragg knocked on the door. There was no answer. He was about to beat a tattoo on it, when there was the sound of a key turning in the lock. The door opened to reveal a slim, good-looking woman in her mid-thirties.

'I am afraid that my husband is out visiting,' she said with an apologetic smile. 'And I have no idea of when he will return.'

'That's all right, Mrs Calder,' Bragg said cheerfully. 'As it happens, it is you we want to see.'

'Me?' she said in surprise.

'We are police officers. We are making enquiries into the death of Professor Edward Dawson.'

Concern and alarm flickered across her face.

'May we come in?'

She smiled disarmingly. 'Yes, of course. I

will get us some coffee.'

'No, ma'am. We just want a quick chat.'

She turned and led the way into a large sitting-room. It seemed sparsely furnished, for modern taste; the curtains hung limply at the window. It looked as if every penny had to be counted. Still, such people could look forward to their reward in heaven...

Bragg took a chair opposite her. 'It must get a bit ripe, when the wind is in the wrong direction,' he said cheerfully. 'You being so close to the brewery.'

She looked puzzled. 'Yes, that is certainly true.'

'Could your husband not get a nice country parish?'

'He could do so, officer. But he sees his mission in life as caring for the spiritual needs of the industrious classes.'

'All credit to him, then. I imagine Tyrrell's brewery is in his parish.'

'That is so... And, unlike most members of the clergy, he is prepared to go among the workers there, sharing their troubles, bringing them support and comfort amid the toil.'

'Very creditable,' Bragg said drily. 'So he knows his way about the place?'

'He spends some part of most weekdays there.'

'And you are content with that?'

'But of course! It is William's vocation.'

'I expect he met Professor Dawson there.'

She nodded. 'He has told me that the professor was conducting some experiments at Tyrrell's.'

'And you will have met him also.'

There was a fractional hesitation. 'I suppose that I must have done so... I feel sure that I was introduced to him at a Christmas party there. What a terrible accident to befall him!'

'From what we can gather, ma'am, you knew him a deal better than that!'

'I do not follow you, officer.'

'Well, I doubt if you would be receiving expensive bouquets of flowers, from some-one you had merely shaken hands with.'

She frowned. 'I do not understand what you are implying,' she said.

'I am saying that Edward Dawson has sent you flowers.'

'Occasionally, yes.'

'Frequently ... regularly. And, if it came to it, we could subpoena the florist to swear to it!'

She shook her head in perplexity. 'I cannot understand the purpose of your questions,' she said. 'What have I to do with an accident that occurred in Tyrrell's brewery?'

'Since you were due to meet the dead man this very day, I would have thought the purpose was obvious,' Bragg said. 'How long has your husband been the vicar at St Mark's?'

'For three years only.'

'Where was he before that?'

'He was a chaplain in the army, when I married him.'

'A sanctifier of killing, eh? And that was when?'

'Seven years ago.'

'Any children?'

She bowed her head. 'None,' she said reluctantly.

'Did you not want any?'

'One cannot have everything one wants in life.'

'So you did want children?'

'Of course! But my husband...'

'Go on, ma'am!'

She took a deep breath. 'Before I met him, my husband had served for some years in South Africa, as an army chaplain. He was there when the Boers invaded Natal. He was badly wounded. Even now he is limited in what he can do.'

'He left the army, then?'

'Yes. That is the reason why the bishop gave him this parish.'

'You mean, his wounds?'

'Yes. As you must realise, it is something of a sinecure... Not that I was aware of the situation when I married him.'

'What situation are you talking about now?'

She looked out of the window for a space, then: 'He was with the troops at the battle of Majuba Hill,' she said. 'The Boers were using mortar bombs against the trenches. A bomb burst in the trench where my husband was sheltering... His wounds left him less than a man.'

Bragg frowned 'Are you saying he could

123

not be a proper husband to you?'

She dropped her head. 'Yes... But it was not so much that. Had I known, I might... It was his cold assumption that it should not matter. That this was a burden he was entitled to foist on me, without my knowledge and consent.'

'So, when Dawson came along, you decided to get your own back?'

'No! It was nothing as cold-blooded as you make it sound. Edward was vital, amusing, distinguished. I admit that I was flattered; but I told myself that this was merely a social game. Even when we became lovers, I felt I was justified – until my conscience began to prick.'

'From the number of times he sent you flowers, it didn't prick very hard,' Bragg said drily.

'I know I did wrong!' she exclaimed. 'But I had been wronged in my turn! Even so, I tried to end the affair; till Edward hinted that he could easily make my husband aware of what had happened.'

'And, where would you and Dawson meet?'

She dropped her head. 'In a hotel in King's Cross, which facilitates such liaisons.'

'It all sounds a bit seedy,' Bragg said. 'Particularly for a vicar's wife.'

She flinched. 'I had been grievously wronged by the man who should have been my husband, my lover, my friend... I felt justified! I suppose I saw it as a kind of...'

'Revenge?' Bragg suggested.

'Well, if you must have it so, yes! But I did try... I began to realise how stupid I was; that to Edward I was little more than a trophy; that, had I not been a vicar's wife, he might have had not the slightest interest in me.'

'You mean he was a bit unnatural?'

'I felt that cuckolding a Church of England vicar in some way increased the satisfaction he obtained from our meetings. I did try to end it. I felt my husband was becoming suspicious; he had begun to ask where I had been. When I told Edward that we must stop seeing each other, he told me his price ... the last meeting must be here – in my husband's bed. I refused. Then he threatened to inform my husband of what had been taking place. He said it would be appropriate to make an act of confession to a parish priest.'

'So you agreed?'

She gazed out of the window. 'To gratify that vile man's whim I would have sent the servants off, today, and submitted to his lust ... defiled my husband's bed – for someone not worthy of licking his boots!'

'Except that, in the meantime, he was murdered. Are you still saying your husband knew nothing?' Bragg asked quietly.

She was silent for some moments. Then she began to speak in a quiet, remote voice. 'I suppose that William might have felt a change in my attitude towards him,' she said. 'I could not but be affected. There was a new dimension to my life. I became resentful of the way I had been trapped; aware of what might have been... Then, a month ago, he challenged me. He had seen the flowers. He went through the contents of the dustbin, and found the florist's paper and card... I could not pretend that I had bought them myself. At first I refused to tell him. But he threatened to go to the florist and make a scene... So I capitulated.'

'You told him Dawson had sent them?'

'I said that I thought it must be he.'

'You don't know if he confronted Dawson?'

'No. But I am convinced that he could not have caused Edward's death. Whatever else he might be, or not be, William is a man of God.'

'Yes,' Bragg said drily. 'But, through the ages, some unlikely things have been done in the name of gods. If I were you, I would be taking a long holiday, as far from here as I could get!'

Manor Park cemetery looked a treat, Bragg thought. The sun was shining, the gravelled paths newly raked, the grass between the graves cut short. Mind you, it cost a small fortune to sleep out eternity here. You should get the full treatment.

Morton hurried up. 'I gather that the Dawson burial is to be in the next section,' he said. 'Probably those people, over there, are waiting for the hearse.'

'Then we will join them.'

As they picked their way through the graves, Bragg could see the hearse approaching down one of the avenues. Black plumes nodded on the horses' heads, black-clad mutes paced solemnly before it. The other carriages had stopped a little way off, their occupants were walking behind the hearse, heads bowed. Mrs Dawson was leaning on the arm of a middle-aged man, her face veiled. Near the end of the avenue, a parson in cassock and surplice was waiting by an open grave. It must be a high-class funeral, Bragg thought sourly. They had even gone to the trouble of concealing the excavated soil with a green tarpaulin. Was the grieving widow supposed to think that Dawson would be whisked up to heaven? That he would not be six foot under, within an hour of her leaving the cemetery? The parson had started intoning bits from the Bible.

'Man that is born of woman hath but a short time to live and is full of misery.'

Well, Dawson's time had been a deal shorter than he had expected. But it had hardly been miserable. There was a lot to be said for getting knocked off in your prime. No waning of the senses, no physical decline.

'*Thou knowest, Lord the secrets of our hearts...*'

There were plenty of secrets among this lot. Mrs Dawson for one. Whose arm was she leaning on? He was certainly very solicitous.

The undertakers' men were lowering the coffin into the grave. Mrs Dawson bent down, picked up a handful of earth and dropped it on top of the coffin. Several men followed suit – Lubbock, no doubt representing the brewery; Turnbury and Waller, his former students; some Bragg did not recognise.

'*Earth to earth, ashes to ashes, dust to dust.*'

Bragg wondered why Dawson was entitled to a sure and certain hope of resurrection to eternal life. He had been a selfish womaniser... But, if anything, the Rev. William Calder had been more callous; from what his wife said, anyway. But how far was she embroidering the truth?

The parson was muttering on ... resurrection ... blessing ... the kingdom prepared for you. How many of those present believed in this mumbo-jumbo? Bragg wondered. He, himself, did not expect to see his young wife and her baby on some far-distant resurrection day. What was the point of promising it?

'In my flesh shall I see God.'

If it meant anything at all, she would still be a young woman, with a baby in her arms. He would be an old man. Yet, if you were only going to be a spirit, there was damn little point in meeting in the hereafter.

People were beginning to move away. The parson was mumbling solicitously to Mrs Dawson. Her response was hidden by her veil, but presumably she would have the grace to cry a little. Bragg went over to Lubbock.

'A good turn-out,' he remarked.

'There will be more at the memorial service,' Lubbock said gruffly.

'Who is the man with Mrs Dawson?'

'Charles Anscombe, the banker.'

'I see. And the Eldridges are here. Finance

and the law!'

'Dawson was very well thought of.'

'Indeed! Tell me, who is the man talking to Waller and Turnbury?'

Lubbock turned. 'That's Albert Hunt. Representing the college, I should think. Will you be going to the reception?'

'Reception?'

'Yes – if that is what you call it. Mrs Dawson has arranged for a snack at the Railway Inn, for those that want it.'

Bragg smiled. 'That is good of her. But somehow I hardly think it would be proper.'

When Bragg went in to Old Jewry, next morning, the desk sergeant beckoned him over.

'The Commissioner was looking for you, yesterday afternoon,' he said.

'I was at a funeral.'

'Huh! Like as not you will be at your own funeral, if you don't go in and report to him.'

'I'm busy. Tell him you haven't seen me.'

'Not on your life, Joe. You can't have it every way!'

Bragg sighed. 'Oh, well. I expect I can think of something to say that will satisfy him.'

'No doubt. But do it now.'

'All right. Is Morton in?'

'Half an hour ago.'

'All, the energy of youth!'

Bragg went down the corridor, knocked on the Commissioner's door and went in.

Sir William looked up from a document, gestured irritably towards a chair and went on reading. Finally he tossed the papers into his out-tray and leaned back with a frown.

'This Dawson case,' he said stiffly. 'It is now Thursday; five days after his death, and you appear to have discovered nothing.'

'Morton and I have covered a lot of ground, sir,' Bragg said confidingly. 'But I will admit that we have had to retrace our steps somewhat, if you understand what I mean.'

'No, Bragg, I do not understand what you mean! And without understanding, I cannot be expected to give you guidance.'

'Indeed, sir. I was going to come to see you this morning, anyway... As you will remember, we were investigating Dawson's death on the basis that it was an accident. Which is what it looked like. Only, you said we should not ignore the possibility that it was something more serious.'

'Did I?'

'Yes, sir, you did. And you were right. I went to the mortuary, to find out what Professor Burney thought about it. He is convinced it was murder. He will have reported as much to the coroner. So I thought it best to go over the ground again. Sir Rufus doesn't suffer fools gladly, as you know.'

The Commissioner shifted uncomfortably in his chair. 'I see,' he said. 'Yes, Bragg. But have you identified anyone remotely likely to have committed the crime? The academic world does not present itself as a hotbed of murder.'

'You wouldn't think so, would you, sir? But there are rivalries there, the same as anywhere. For instance, we went to the funeral yesterday – the interment at Manor Park cemetery. Beside the family, and a couple of ex-students, there was another man from the college. A senior lecturer, name of Hunt.'

'Was that so surprising?'

'Well, yes. In a way it was. I mean, there is going to be a big memorial service, next week sometime. All the big nobs from the college will be there, in their gowns and what not. It seemed odd, to us, that Hunt should intrude on what should have been a quiet family occasion.'

'Hmm... I see what you mean, Bragg. But where does that take us?'

'Not very far, sir... Except we hear that Hunt was in the running, when Dawson was made a professor.'

'I see.'

'And rumour has it that Hunt will get the vacant chair.'

'Chair?'

'Professorship, sir.'

'Ah, yes, of course... So, clearly he must come under suspicion.'

'Yes, sir. The trouble is, we are not dealing with your ordinary, run-of-the-mill bludger here. We have to tread delicately; and it takes time.'

'Indeed, Bragg. We cannot allow a suspect's social status to hinder our investigation of the crime. But clearly it must, to some extent, dictate our approach... Yes.'

'So you would advise us to see this Hunt man?'

The Commissioner shifted uneasily in his chair. 'From what you say, he would seem to have a motive for this murder. It would appear, therefore, to be our duty to investigate any role he might have had in Dawson's death. But I feel we should not be too precipitate. After all, many people aspire to preferment that they are never likely to achieve.'

'Indeed, sir. But we think that, when Dawson was appointed, Hunt may have been tipped the wink that he would be next.'

'I see ... yes. Very well. Investigate the matter by all means; but I expect you to be discreet.'

'I don't know how we got ourselves lumbered with a Commissioner as indecisive as Sir William Sumner,' Bragg remarked, as they strolled towards

University College. 'But then, I wonder how he ever got to the rank of Lieutenant-Colonel!'

Morton laughed. 'In my father's view, not having fought a major war since Waterloo, the army is more of a gentlemen's club than a serious fighting force. And the debacle in the Crimea seems to bear him out.'

'Well, he should know, if anybody does. But that was forty years ago. And it was not the soldiers that let us down, but inept generals... Come to think of it, the cap does fit! And we are the poor bloody infantry. So we watch each other's back on this one.'

When they reached the Corinthian portico of University College, they were directed to a staircase at the far end of the building. Hunt's room was not as poky as Turnbury's. A senior lecturer was visibly more important than a junior one. There were even a few ornaments here. Given the presence of a girl typewriter, it could have been as pleasant as the room of any City businessman. But the man behind the desk was not out of that mould. He had taken off his frock coat, and was sitting shirt-sleeved in the breeze from the window. At close quarters he was good-looking, with a high forehead and firm jaw. He looked up with a frown as they entered.

'City police!' Bragg said, waving his warrant-card. 'We saw you at Dawson's funeral.'

'Indeed?'

'Yes, sir. Do you mind if we sit down?'

'If you must.' His demeanour was puzzled rather than irritated, Morton thought. Yet certainly not surprised.

'Not many there from the college,' Bragg said amiably.

Hunt shrugged. 'It is the long vacation,' he said. 'But, of course, there will be quite a crowd at the memorial service.'

'Then, why were you there?'

'I had known Dawson for many years. We were fellow students here, longer ago than I care to remember!' His smile was disarming.

'I expect that applies to a lot of people,' Bragg said.

Hunt pursed his lips. 'Not so many as you would think, officer.'

'And, did you study the same subjects?'

'No. My field is thermodynamics.'

Bragg smiled. 'I won't ask what that is, sir. I doubt if I would understand. But I gather that you did some work at Tyrrell's brewery, some time ago.'

Hunt cocked his head on one side, considering. 'I suppose it could be six months ago,' he said. 'I was advising on a new system. As it happens, it was Dawson who mentioned to Tyrrell's that I would be able to help them.'

'I see. So you know your way around the brewery?'

Hunt smiled. 'Unless they have radically altered the layout of the plant – which is unlikely!'

'So you and Dawson got on well – if he was putting work in your way?'

'As well as two colleagues working in very different fields can do, I suppose.'

'And how do you rate him?'

Hunt raised his eyebrows. 'By what measure? As a man? As a scientist? As a teacher?'

'I am sure that we would value your

judgement in every field, sir.'

Hunt laughed. 'There is a certain arrogance in every teacher,' he said. 'But I would never sit in judgement on the work of a fellow academic. That would be giving far too many hostages to fortune!'

'It would only be for our guidance,' Bragg said.

Hunt became serious. 'I think that, on any assessment, Dawson was a brilliant scholar. He was at the top of his particular tree. I am surprised that he was not lured away by some Oxbridge college, or American university. Except that his wife's family have an inordinate amount of wealth; and she refused to forsake London for provincial surroundings, wherever they might be.'

'Did that create tension between them?'

'I doubt it. Dawson himself was a metropolitan creature. And he would have received no greater academic acclaim, had he been teaching at Harvard.'

'I see.' Bragg paused, then: 'I gather that you are next in line for being made a professor,' he said. 'So Dawson's loss would be your gain.'

Hunt was suddenly watchful. 'I admit that I have some modest aspirations in that direction,' he said amiably. 'But I doubt if my time has come. There are other senior lecturers whose tenure exceeds mine.'

Bragg smiled. 'You must realise that we have to consider every possibility, however outlandish it might seem. Would you mind telling us where you were on Saturday afternoon?'

'Not at all officer. I was at Lord's cricket ground, from ten o'clock in the morning until six o'clock in the evening.'

'Watching the cricket, were you, sir?'

'Indeed I was.'

'Will there be anyone who can vouch for that?'

'I doubt it. I was unaccompanied, and unfortunate enough to be surrounded by a sea of Kentish supporters!'

'Bad luck that! Was there any particular piece of play you can remember?'

Hunt smiled. 'Indeed there is! One of their batsmen, a man called Morton, struck the most stupendous six, over long on, that I have ever seen. That stroke almost made up for Middlesex's defeat!'

'Well, that will be all, for the moment,' Bragg said amiably. 'But, if you remember anything that might help us, I would be glad if you would let us know at Old Jewry.'

Hunt smiled. 'You may rely on that, officer,' he said.

Once outside the building, Bragg slowed to a stroll.

'What do you think of him, lad?' he asked.

'Very self-contained; one might say that he had a touch of suppressed excitement.'

'Maybe. But because he can see promotion in the offing, it does not mean he would murder to get it.'

'No. And there would be other candidates, from different disciplines.'

'Yes... And he certainly was at the cricket match, because he saw that six of yours. Though, to my mind, only a twit would go to a cricket match on his own.'

Morton smiled. 'I would not place too much reliance on that, sir,' he said. 'The account of the match in Monday's *Daily Telegraph* made mention of that shot, even using the same adjective.'

141

'Stupendous?'

'Yes, sir. Hardly a coincidence, one would think.'

After a quick lunch in a pub, Bragg and Morton walked to Bouverie Street, near the Temple. It must be useful, Bragg thought sourly, for Tyrrell's to have their solicitor close by. If a workman fell off some scaffolding, Tyrrell could just pop round the corner, and ask how best to deny liability. Fortescue & Blount's brass plate had been polished over so many generations, that its lettering was barely discernible. The clerk in the outer office seemed to go back a good long way, as well. His long face was fringed with white whiskers, and he regarded them suspiciously through rheumy eyes.

'City police,' Bragg said. 'We want to see Mr Eldridge.'

The clerk frowned. 'He is not in,' he said reprovingly.

'Then, where is he?'

'At luncheon.'

'Oh, I see! He goes to luncheon, does he?' Bragg said savagely. 'Where is this? The

Mansion House, or Buckingham Palace?'

'Oh, no. Nothing like that. He generally goes to his club for something light. His wife disapproves of heavy eating in the middle of the day.'

'Ah! Hen-pecked, is he?'

The clerk gave a sly smile. 'Are not we all?' he asked.

'No! We are not! How long is he going to be?'

He glanced at the clock. 'Not long now ... of course, if you wished to make an appointment...'

'Do I look as if I make appointments?' Bragg demanded.

'Since you ask, officer, I doubt if you have the remotest concept of courtesy and good manners. However, if you care to wait I will get one of the typewriters to make you a cup of tea.'

'No, thank you, we have eaten.'

'Then, all I can suggest is that you sit on those chairs, and endeavour to possess your souls in patience.' He turned and went out of the room.

'Came, set and match to the opposition,'

Morton said with a grin.

Bragg snorted and began to pace up and down. He was on the verge of stamping out of the office when the door opened, and a man in his mid-thirties came in. He looked at them quizzically. 'Is anyone looking after you?' he asked. He had a long face, long nose, and eyes that seemed fractionally too close together.

Bragg quelled his irritation. 'We are waiting for Mr Eldridge,' he said.

'I am he! I do apologise. My secretary did not tell me that I had an appointment at two o'clock.'

'You hadn't, sir. We are police officers.'

Eldridge looked at them warily. 'You have, I take it, the usual means of identification?'

Bragg produced his warrant-card. 'We would like to have a word with you.'

Eldridge looked up at the clock. 'Very well, I can give you half an hour. Come this way.'

He led them down a dark corridor, and into a fusty office overlooking a stone-flagged yard. Eldridge was not among the senior partners, Morton thought, if he had

144

to settle for such a room.

Eldridge waved them to chairs, and seated himself behind his desk. To Morton his gestures and mannerisms were exaggerated, as if they were cultivated to disguise an inner diffidence.

'You are the partner that acts for Tyrrell's brewery?' Bragg asked curtly.

'That is the case.'

'How long have you acted for them?'

Eldridge raised his eyebrows. 'Since my father died ... I literally slipped into his chair.'

'And Tyrrell's were happy about that, were they?'

He frowned. 'I have never received any intimation to the contrary.'

'Hmm...' Bragg put his ill temper from him. 'Are they a good firm to be connected with?' he asked amiably.

Eldridge smiled. 'There is a steady stream of work from them, which is both straightforward and remunerative. That would amount to a good client in any solicitor's book!'

'What kind of work?'

'Essentially commercial work, officer.'

'You mean leases of pubs?'

'No. With one or two exceptions, Tyrrell's have never owned public houses. They have traditionally supplied beers to landlord-owned houses. That is not to say that they own no hostelries. But the ownership of licensed premises has been incidental, rather than a result of policy.'

'Meaning what?'

'Suppose that the landlord of an inn has fallen on hard times; to such an extent that he cannot pay the money he owes for beers already supplied. Old Thomas Tyrrell adopted the solution of buying the premises and leasing them back. So the debtor would clear his debt and continue to trade; on the basis, of course, that all the beers sold were bought from Tyrrell's! The practice has proved so successful, that it has been adopted by other breweries.'

'So you are drawing up the leases for the pubs?'

'Yes. Also chasing debtors, and dealing with general liability work. But, at the moment, I am heavily involved with the

proposed purchase of a brewery in Dorchester.

'I see. Tell me, do you do their insurance
work?'

Eldridge shook his head. 'I imagine I
would only become involved, if it were
necessary to obtain counsel's opinion on
some matter.'

'Ah. So what about this Dawson
business?'

Eldridge tensed, then leaned back to
disguise it. 'That was a straightforward
industrial accident. I would have thought
that it was covered by the general insurance
policy.'

'But he was not an employee of Tyrrell's.'

'True. However, he was experimenting
there by permission of the directors ... An
interesting point! It will certainly bear
consideration, officer.'

Bragg paused, then: 'I was surprised not to
see you at the cemetery, sir,' he said.

Eldridge frowned. 'I hardly ever met the
man,' he said.

'Odd, that,' Bragg remarked. 'George
Tyrrell thought he was a feather in their cap.

Put them on a level with Whitbread's and their Pasteur.'

'Well, however that be, I barely knew him.'

'Hmm...' Bragg sniffed. 'Well, if you barely knew him, your wife knew him barely... I know it's bad taste to be flippant about such matters, sir, but your wife has admitted that she and Dawson were lovers.'

Eldridge was staring at them, a dazed look on his face.

'You knew that, of course,' Bragg said.

'I did not know it!'

'There is none so blind as those who will not see, eh? She told us about it readily enough.'

'She ... she is apt to embroider the truth for her own amusement.'

'But she would hardly invent a thing like that.'

'My wife is a self-assured socialite. She is capable of doing anything which will give her a moment's pleasure or amusement. She comes from a large family, and is accustomed to holding her own... In any case, I hardly see how this can impinge on the accident that befell Dawson.'

'Accident?' Bragg pursed his lips. 'Did I not tell you, sir? The pathologist, Professor Burney, is convinced it was murder...Where were you on the afternoon of Saturday the twenty-second of June?'

Eldridge looked dazed. He shook his head slowly. 'I cannot believe it,' he muttered.

'Where were you?'

'I was here... I needed peace and quiet to study the documents on the Dorchester brewery. There are extensive legal ramifications.'

'Can anyone vouch that you were here?'

'No. Of course not.'

Bragg got to his feet. 'Then, if you weren't one yourself, I would say it was time you got yourself a good lawyer.'

On leaving Eldridge, Bragg and Morton went along to the brewery. They found Lubbock in his office, going through a pile of invoices. He looked up as they entered.

'You again?' he asked disagreeably.

'Just a quick chat,' Bragg said.

'That is a contradiction in terms, as you bloody well know!'

'We have been to see Eldridge, your solicitor.'

'I don't have solicitors!'

'Very well then, the solicitor to Thomas Tyrrell Ltd... Is he always as wound up as that?'

Lubbock frowned. 'He has his problems,' he said curtly.

'You mean, the one he is married to?'

'If you like.'

'Has she always been flighty?'

Lubbock glared at him. 'I don't gossip,' he said.

Bragg nodded his acquiescence. 'How far have you got with the Dorchester brewery purchase? From what Eldridge said, he has been doing a lot of work on it.'

'Then he is way ahead of himself! It's a good business, I'll not deny that. But the old biddy that owns it is sticking out for every last penny it is worth.'

'That's not unreasonable, is it?'

'No. But she could push us too hard.'

'Right ... I get the feeling, sir, that not everybody was happy to have Dawson researching at Tyrrell's.'

150

Lubbock frowned. 'For my money, he was a bloody nuisance. He was just out to make a name for himself, putting fancy names to things we had known for generations! But for him, I could have replaced that little vat, put in a three thousand one – maybe that other one in there also. That mounts up to a lot of extra beer in a year!'

'More money in your pocket? Bigger dividends?'

'I don't have shares,' he said curtly.

'But you are a director?'

'I am, because they couldn't run this place without me! But, when it comes to sharing out the profits, oh no! Not for the likes of me! You have to have been at the right school – Eton and suchlike.'

'So Dawson was something of a thorn in your flesh?'

Lubbock snorted. 'Would have been, if anyone had taken notice of him... One day he came in, large as life, back from some jollification on the Continent. He insisted on addressing a meeting of the directors. Full of the notion that we should use cultivated strains of yeast from laboratories, he was; instead of using part of the head from one brew to ferment another... All moonshine!'

Bragg paused to let Lubbock's indignation subside, then: 'Do women come here much? I mean, apart from the trollops that Dick White mentioned.'

'Over the last few years we have allowed organised parties to look round. A brewery is a dangerous place, so they have got to be properly controlled. For my part, I would stop it. But I am told that it is as good as a score of advertisements.'

'And a proportion of these visitors would be women?'

'A few of them.'

'And, of course, there are the parties at Christmas for the staff and so on.'

'Yes. And the "so on" are getting more and more every year.'

'The guests would include Dawson and his wife?'

'Last Christmas they came, I do know. And, of course, they were here a month ago.'

'Really?'

'Yes. There was a party to celebrate

George Tyrrell's twenty years as chairman. Big do, that was. Everybody remotely connected with the company was here, wives and all.'

'I see. And that would include the Eldridges, the Dawsons? What about Anscombe, the banker?'

'He was here... Even a chap called Hunt from the college; and he'd only done some drawings for a new plant layout.'

'Well, I suppose twenty years as chairman is something of a milestone.'

'It's more than they will do for me, when I retire, I can tell you! An engraved tankard will be my mark. But who makes the profits for them?'

'The workers, of course,' Bragg said with a grin. 'You are lucky. In my job we are just looked on as a damn nuisance, an un-necessary expense.'

Lubbock scowled. 'Well you are, aren't you?' he said.

Catherine floated serenely up the grand staircase at Lanesborough House. This great mansion seemed to have been a formative influence on her life. Her own parents lived comparatively modestly, despite the fashionable villa in Park Lane. But this house was at the centre of the beau monde. Lady Lanesborough was one of the great society hostesses. As Catherine's godmother, she had set herself to be her mentor and guide. She had introduced her to a succession of would-be suitors – eligible in society's terms, but vapid and shallow in her eyes. In truth, the only young man she had admired enough to marry was James Morton. She touched the engagement ring, now secure on her finger. No one could possibly be happier than she was at this moment! On the landing she glanced up at the portrait of Lady Lanesborough, painted by her father when he first came to London – before she was even born! It had been the talisman of his success. Society hostesses had flocked to his studio – he had become famous! Yet he and, particularly, her mother had kept their feet firmly on the ground. Her mother was sprung from Winchester gentry. When they were first married, she had kept house for herself, without any servants. Still could, if need be. And she had made sure that Catherine had a similar grounding. It would be daunting, of course, to run Ashwell Priory. Her mother-in-law to be was a resolute, resourceful woman. Woe betide the servant who skimped her work and tried to outface her. She could not emulate that. It was partly Lady Morton's background. She had been the daughter of the American ambassador in London. The rigid social hierarchy of the English country house was anathema to her. She could easily have been submerged, Catherine thought, with her husband serving abroad for years at a time. Certainly any English woman, in her position, would have become a hostage to the whims of her servants. But Charlotte Morton had more than met the challenge. It was an example she would have to follow, try to emulate. Though, when the time came, James would be by her side. They would be facing the future together.

Catherine went into the drawing-room. The last of the visitors were taking their leave, amid effusive protestations. The debased coinage of social intercourse,

Catherine thought, then mentally chided herself. Society could not exist if its members were even a quarter honest!... It was the prospect of being transplanted into a country environment that was making her over-critical, she thought. And certainly, when immured in that great house in Kent, she would long for the lights of London, for the theatres, for the humble London cabs that could whisk you away to your heart's desire... Except that James was all she desired, and he would be in Ashwell also.

She accepted a cup of tea from a maid, then loitered in a corner. Her design was to wait until Lady Lanesborough was alone; not to become involved in socialising. It seemed as if half of London had peered at her engagement ring, muttered platitudes, then gone off to report to the other half! But that was setting altogether too high a value on herself and her doings. It was mere politeness, the ordinary coinage of a civilised society. And within six months of her leaving it, society would have forgotten her... Irked by this unflattering conclusion, she looked around her. There was a group of ladies conversing animatedly by the door. On the other side of the room, her godmother was chatting with an old crony, Mrs Gerald de Trafford. Catherine put down her cup and crossed over to them.

Lady Lanesborough looked up. 'I had begun to think that you had forsaken me, child,' she said reproachfully. 'I have not set eyes on you for weeks!' She seized her hand. 'Is this the definitive engagement ring?' she asked.

Catherine laughed. 'My one, only and final engagement ring! Determined upon after great agony of soul and body!'

Her godmother sniffed. 'Well, if you were content to do as others do, and eschew your silly journalising, you would not get into such scrapes.'

'Where are you going to live, after your marriage?' Mrs de Trafford asked eagerly.

'In London. Somewhere on the borders of the City would be convenient for both of us.'

Lady Lanesborough frowned. 'They are intent on continuing with their careers!' she said censoriously. 'It is the height of absurdity! Not least, that each of them is competent to discharge far greater responsibilities than their present occupations entail. In fact, they will be paying out to their servants, more than they earn between them!'

'And what would you have us do, godmother?' Catherine asked teasingly.

'Why, take your place in society, of course!'

'But it is society's edicts that are delaying our marriage. James only accepted the necessity for postponement, with a very ill grace. I will give no hostages to fortune!'

Mrs de Trafford leaned forward conspiratorially 'What kind of residence are you looking for?' she asked.

'A house or an apartment; it does not matter at this stage,' Catherine said. 'I would like it to be tiny, so that we could dispense with servants. But I fear it is a romantic ideal my cooking would rapidly dispel! Of course, James has Mr and Mrs Chambers looking after him at present. I suspect he wants them to stay on for a transitional period, while we adjust to married life.'

'But you would not want that, surely?'

Catherine shrugged. 'As I said, James is still outraged at the year's delay imposed on us. I do not intend to throw down any gauntlets at this stage! In any case, I know the Chamberses, and I think it would work very well.'

Lady Lanesborough shook her head. 'I do not understand what you young people want out of life,' she complained. 'You seem to take delight in doing the very opposite of what your parents want; of what they did at your age!'

Catherine smiled. 'As you well know, my mother married a penniless artist. They lived in a tiny cottage, just the two of them. And she served in a shop, to augment their slender resources. I am proud of that!'

'Yes, no doubt. But he was exceptionally talented.'

'Well, I shall not need to serve in a shop for my husband. But I do want to continue my own career ... which is one reason why I came to see you this afternoon.'

Mrs de Trafford leaned forward eagerly. 'What has happened?' she asked. 'I have heard nothing about anyone for weeks!'

Catherine smiled. 'I have no scandal for you! But I did wonder if you knew anything about the Tyrrell family.'

'Tyrrell?' Lady Lanesborough echoed. 'Do we know any Tyrrells?'

'They own the brewery in the City.'

The anticipation faded from her godmother's face. 'Oh, those Tyrrells,' she said. 'But they are tradesmen! Wealthy tradesmen, I believe... But certainly not people of quality. You could not expect us to know of them!'

5

Next morning Bragg and Morton were in the porch of St Mark's, Whitefriars, at half-past eight. Through the open door, they could hear the low murmur of people saying the responses. The voice of the celebrant was firm and confident.

'Funny the wrong ideas you can get, lad,' Bragg observed. 'After what happened to Calder, I expected him to sound more like a treble than a bass.'

'From what Mrs Calder told us, he behaves more like a treble!'

'Now then, lad,' Bragg said reprovingly, 'there's no call for that! Keep an open mind; she might have been feeding us a lot of nonsense.'

'Sorry, sir... Though my impression of Mrs Calder is that she was extraordinarily frank and truthful.'

'Hmm... What we should be asking

ourselves, is whether he had it in him to club Dawson over the head and drown him.'

'Physically, I would say most certainly. He seems to lead an active life.'

'Yes. But does someone, wounded as Calder was, lose a man's natural aggression?'

'I have no idea, sir... His character was obviously fully formed. I cannot see that it would be altered in any great degree by his wounds.'

'No... And we have a man who is used to handing down penances. He would have no trouble justifying himself ... Hello, the congregation is coming out.'

Somehow there were more of them than Morton had expected; and a good proportion of them men. Even though most of them were past working age, it seemed surprising.

'Come on, lad.' Bragg led the way into the church.

Calder was in the chancel, carrying the communion chalice and paten towards the vestry. He had a long, beaky nose and prominent chin. He looked like Mr Punch,

Bragg thought uncharitably.

'Good morning!' he greeted them. 'You were not in time for the service! We have been celebrating the day of St Peter the Apostle a day early. Being a City church, there would be very few communicants on a Saturday morning. So we gave ourselves a dispensation to observe it today!'

'We are police officers,' Bragg said. 'We have come to see you about the death of Edward Dawson.'

Calder seemed not to have heard him. He sniffed twice, then began to walk slowly towards the vestry. They followed him. Once inside he stooped to open the door of a safe. He polished the chalice, then the paten, with a soft cloth, placed them in the safe and locked the door. He bowed his head briefly, then turned to Bragg.

'Edward Dawson was not a parishioner of mine,' he said briskly. 'I had no duty of care in respect of him. But I had seen him, on occasion, in Tyrrell's brewery ... It is in my parish, you understand.'

'Were you aware that he was murdered?'

'Murdered? No. Poor fellow! God grant

his soul repose.'

'You knew that your wife was involved with him?'

Calder's composure was not ruffled. 'She did confess as much to me,' he said. 'My wife is deeply troubled, officer... She also told me that you called at the vicarage and cross-questioned her. I did not expect to find such reprehensible conduct in the City police.'

'I would say we just had a chat, sir,' Bragg said mildly. 'We were more of a shoulder to cry on, if you understand me.'

'It is my function to bring succour to the souls in this parish, officer. And that includes my wife.'

'In the ordinary way, I am sure that is right. But, from what she says, you have not been able to bring her the succour she wants.'

Calder stared coldly at Bragg. 'She could aspire to no higher vocation than to serve God, and assist me to care for His flock in St Mark's parish.'

'But you wronged her, by any measure.'

Calder frowned at him. 'I prayed about it,

before I proposed marriage. I am sure I received God's blessing!'

'Your wife feels you betrayed her, you know that.'

'Women, on occasion, do become overwrought, officer.'

'That was the main reason she became Dawson's mistress. I take it she has told you about that.'

Calder looked down his nose disdainfully. 'She has confessed it,' he said. 'And I have given her absolution.'

'You've what?' Bragg exclaimed. 'You were the cause of it all! In the ordinary course, she would not have looked twice at Dawson.'

Calder gave a contemptuous smile. 'You appear to have become a considerable expert in my wife's doings and opinions,' he said. 'But then, she never had difficulty in recruiting a coterie of people to commiserate with her... I did what I did because God was guiding me. Jennifer has been privileged to tread the path of righteousness with me.'

'And when she strayed from it?'

'Why, I forgave her, of course.'

'That's not the way she told it to us. I reckon you practically drove her into Dawson's arms.'

Calder stared coldly at him. 'Whatever you or I think and say is now academic. Dawson will have been before the Judgement Seat; reward and punishment will have been meted out, as to all sinners.'

'It is not academic to me!' Bragg said wrathfully. 'I am going to catch his killer.'

'Then, you will have to look elsewhere.'

'I see... Where were you, on the afternoon of June the twenty-second?'

'I was out and about in my parish, ministering to my flock.'

'There are not many of them about, on a Saturday afternoon. It should be easy for you to remember who you saw.'

Calder gave a tolerant smile. 'In this parish it is possible to see most of my flock, by the simple expedient of walking down the street. I prefer informality, spontaneity. We are like a large family, officer. We do not make appointments, hold conferences. We just live the Christian life together.'

166

Bragg snorted. 'So you didn't happen to be living the Christian life in Tyrrell's brewery that afternoon; and give the man who was tupping your wife a bang over the head, that sent him to eternity?'

Calder looked calmly at him. 'No, officer. As God is my maker and judge.'

Bragg and Morton strolled to the coroner's court in Golden Lane. It was approaching five years, since Sir Rufus Stone had been appointed coroner for the City of London. His predecessor had been an unprepossessing medical man, who had manipulated the judicial process in connection with the sudden death of a friend. When the man proved to have been murdered, the position of Dr Primrose became untenable, and he resigned his office. As a result, the newspapers had got hold of the story. The cosy, oligarchical government of the City had been attacked. Charges of corruption, nepotism, venality were freely bandied about. So much so, that the reputation of the City's institutions had begun to suffer. It was rumoured that the

Governor of the Bank of England had demanded a public gesture, which would demonstrate the determination of the authorities to restore the City's credibility. Certainly they had gone outside the City for their new coroner. Sir Rufus Stone's eminence at the bar was undisputed, his scorn of political jobbery well known, his independence of thought manifest. Although he had accepted the office reluctantly, he had set about his duties with a vigour and determination that would brook neither interference nor slackness. 'I have been brought in to cleanse the Augean stables,' he would declaim. 'And, by God, cleanse them I will.'

Sir Rufus's high-handed methods had frequently raised the hackles of self-important City personages. It was said they were biding their time; that he only had to put a foot wrong, and they would be rid of him. If he knew of the rumour, he disregarded it. The City fathers had pleaded with him to rescue them from opprobrium, he would say, and he had set his own terms. These included a lofty disregard for the convenience of everyone but himself.

The coroner's desk was on a high dais, with the City of London's coat of arms resplendent in scarlet and gold behind it. To the left, the coroner's clerk was swearing in the jury. On the right was the witness-box. Bragg and Morton installed themselves at one end of a pew-like bench.

At precisely ten o'clock, the clerk rapped on his desk to call those present to order. The coroner came billowing out of a side room and ascended the dais. He glared about him until the hum of conversation had subsided, bowed to the court and sat down. He adjusted his wig, glanced at his papers, then nodded to his clerk.

The clerk jumped to his feet. 'In the matter of Edward Dawson deceased,' he announced, and sat down again.

Sir Rufus leaned forward and directed a wolfish smile at a young man sitting beside the clerk. 'Mr Farnaby,' he said, 'I understand that you are in attendance to represent the interests – whatever they might be – of the Atlas Assurance Company.'

Farnaby got diffidently to his feet. 'Yes, your honour... There is a large insurance policy, which may be activated as a result of the decision of this court.'

'Very well... The court will take evidence of identity,' he said.

An usher approached a man sitting in the front row. He stood and was led to the witness-box. It was Hunt. The usher placed a Bible in his hand, and he took the oath with the bravura of a seasoned lecturer.

'What is your name?' Sir Rufus asked.

'Albert Hunt, as in Hunt on Thermodynamics.'

The coroner's eyes narrowed. 'My court is not a forum for self-publicity,' he said sternly. 'Any repetition, and I will have you arrested for contempt... What is your address?'

Hunt looked cowed. 'University College London.'

'You reside on the college premises?'

'No, sir.'

'Then, what is your private address?'

Hunt hesitated. 'Seven, Wheelwright Street, Islington,' he said.

Sir Rufus furrowed his brow. 'Ah, yes,' he said with a wolfish smile. 'Just by Pentonville prison, I know it.'

Hunt looked mortified, he licked his lips nervously.

'Have you been shown the body of a man, by the mortuary attendants?' the coroner asked.

'I have.'

'And did you recognise the deceased?'

'Yes, sir. He was a colleague of mine at the college – Professor Edward Dawson.'

Sir Rufus nodded. 'Very well, you may stand down.'

Hunt stumbled down the steps of the witness-box and left the court. As he did so, Catherine came in, bobbed a brief curtsey to the coroner and went over to the press-box. She looked very competent and self-contained, Morton thought. How would such a confirmed city-dweller cope with an unstimulating life as chatelaine of Ashworth Priory? However good her intentions, however determined she was, she could only find it limiting – boring even.

'I will now take evidence of discovery.'

Jack Thompson was ushered to the witness-box. He seemed uneasy in his starched collar and best jacket. He mumbled the oath hesitantly, then grasped the edge of the witness-box with both hands.

'How did you come to find the body of Mr Dawson?' Sir Rufus asked with surprising gentleness.

'I was...' He swallowed hard. 'I was on afternoon shift at the brewery...'

'That is Tyrrell's brewery, I assume.'

'Yes, your honour ... I had occ ... I ... went into the old vat house to get a ladder. There are two vats in there, a big one and a little one... And I saw his ladder slipped over, and his feet sticking out over the edge.'

Sir Rufus smiled. 'Over the edge of one vat only, I presume.'

'Yes, sir. The little one. Mr Tyrrell let him take samples from the vat ... he was some sort of scientist.'

'So, what action did you take?'

'I ran and got Mr White, the foreman. Then we went and got him out... But he was dead.'

172

'Did you try to revive him?'

'We held him up by his ankles, to drain him out; but it was no good.'

'Did you expect to see him there, on a Saturday afternoon?' the coroner asked.

'He would come and go as he pleased, sir. It wasn't proper work, if you understand me. He would be there any old time.'

'Quite. Now, the jury will want to know the size of the vat.'

'It was fourteen feet high, sir, and ten across.'

'Would it be true to say that his body was floating on top of the vat's contents?'

'Yes, sir. There was wort in there that was fermenting.'

'I see... We do not wish to go further into the technicalities of the brewing process than we need, Mr Thompson.'

The coroner turned towards the jury. 'Have you any questions for this witness?' he asked.

There was a general shaking of heads.

'Then, thank you, Mr Thompson. You may stand down.'

Thompson hurried from the court, a

relieved smile on his face.

'Call Roger Turnbury!'

This was a surprise, Bragg thought. One of the suspects being confronted with the events surrounding the crime. But Turnbury seemed composed enough, as he took the oath.

'I believe, Mr Turnbury, that you were a fellow academic of Professor Dawson,' Sir Rufus remarked.

'Yes, sir. He was my supervisor, when I was studying for my Master of Science degree, which I duly obtained.'

'Are all scientists inveterate self-publicists?' Sir Rufus exclaimed irritably. 'We are concerned here with Edward Dawson, and Edward Dawson only. Please exercise some of the scientific objectivity we are always hearing about!'

Turnbury bowed his head and said nothing.

'Can you tell the court, in general terms, why Professor Dawson needed to conduct experiments in Tyrrell's brewery?'

'Since I am researching in much the same field, yes, I can.'

'Well, then?' Sir Rufus said crossly.

'There are microscopic creatures which can breed in the contents of a vat during fermentation. These bacteria bring about a chemical reaction in the wort, causing it to give off a smell like rotting vegetation. The whole contents of the vat are ruined; which constitutes a considerable financial loss to the brewery.'

'Yes... Well, we do not want to stray from the matter in hand... Is this a common occurrence in breweries?'

'I believe it is, sir. Hence the breweries' willingness to facilitate research.'

'And, where do these bacteria come from?'

'They are all around us. But the most common wort-spoilers – the coliform bacteria – are also found in the intestines of animals and humans. The probability is that the water supply to a brewery becomes contaminated, because it has not been adequately treated.'

There were gasps, a murmur ran round the courtroom.

Sir Rufus glared around him, then swung

back to Turnbury. 'I am sure that you have no intention of sensationalising this matter,' he said sternly. 'But it would be unwise of anyone to attempt to use my court for his own ends.'

Turnbury was visibly shaken. 'I was merely trying to explain the background to Professor Dawson's research,' he said. 'There is nothing new about wort-spoilers; what is new is our increasing understanding of the processes involved... And let me make it clear that there is no possibility of these bacteria infecting human beings, and causing illness in them.'

There was a murmur of relief, instantly quelled by a frown from the coroner.

'You say, Mr Turnbury, that you have worked in the same field as Professor Dawson. Can you shed any light on the probable events surrounding this tragedy?'

Turnbury frowned. 'I can only speculate as to what he was doing at the time ... As fermentation begins, the temperature of the wort – the raw material in the vat – begins to rise. The heat gives a stimulus to the bacteria, which are capable of multiplying at a phenomenal rate. Professor Dawson used to mount a ladder and take samples, from different points over the surface of the vat. He would place those samples in small glass bottles, which he would label appropriately.'

'What do you mean by appropriately?'

'Showing the stage of fermentation reached, and the approximate point on the surface of the vat from which the sample was taken... He would then take the samples back to his laboratory, for microscopic examination.'

At that point Professor Burney bustled into the courtroom and, to his evident relief, Turnbury was allowed to stand down. Burney was called to the witness-box and took the oath.

'Have you carried out a post-mortem examination on the body of Professor Edward Dawson?' Sir Rufus asked.

'Yes, sir. And I must once again make the point, that it would have been infinitely better if the police had called me to the scene,' he said with a trace of petulance. 'Informed intuition is no substitute for actual observation.'

'I am sure that your remarks will be noted,' Sir Rufus said meaningfully. 'Now, are you able to shed any light on the cause of death?'

'Oh, he drowned!' Burney's mouth sagged open in satisfaction. 'I was able to compare the yeast spores taken from the liquid in his lungs, with a specimen I later took from the vat itself. They were identical... As to the time of death, I can be of little assistance to the court. When a body cools in the atmosphere, it does so at a reasonably predictable rate. But this subject had been drowned in a vat of heated liquid.'

'I see.'

'There is also an ancillary matter that I should mention, your honour. There was a fresh contusion, below the right ear.'

'Can you speculate as to the cause?' Sir Rufus asked.

'That is hardly within my function, your honour... It could have been caused by a blow; equally it could have resulted from violent contact with the rim of the vat.'

'Very well. Thank you, Professor Burney.'

The pathologist was about to leave the

witness-stand, when the young barrister sprang to his feet. 'I have some questions for this witness, your honour,' he blurted out.

Sir Rufus frowned. 'Very well,' he said.

Farnaby took a deep breath. 'You are no doubt very experienced in the matter of autopsies,' he remarked.

Burney's loose smile enveloped him. 'Indeed. I have been the police pathologist for the City of London for approaching twenty years. In addition, I am the professor of pathology at St Bartholomew's medical school.'

Farnaby swallowed hard. 'As I told the coroner,' he said, 'I represent the interests of an insurance company. Professor Dawson's life was insured by them for a considerable sum...Would you say, from your experience, that he died of natural causes or not?'

Burney frowned. 'We are in the realm of semantics here,' he said. 'Everyone dies of natural causes in that, when the heart stops, we stop. Death is a natural event.'

'But he did not die in his bed.'

'Mr Farnaby!' Sir Rufus intervened angrily. 'This is an abuse of legal proceedings! I will not have my court turned into a debating chamber. If your instructing solicitor were here, I would have some trenchant observations to make to him!'

Farnaby quailed. 'I ... I apologise to your honour. It was an error of judgement ... I will desist.' He sat down humiliated.

Sir Rufus took out his watch. 'It is now half-past eleven o'clock. I will therefore sum up, to enable the jury to retire before noon. The court officials will arrange for tea and sandwiches to be available in the jury room. The court will reassemble at half-past one, to await the verdict... Does that seem reasonable to everyone?'

He glanced round the courtroom; no one ventured to object.

'Very well... Now, gentlemen of the jury, you are charged with the important and weighty duty of reaching a verdict as to the cause of the death of Edward Dawson. He was a distinguished teacher and scientist. You have heard from a colleague of his – Mr Turnbury – that the deceased used to visit Tyrrell's brewery, for the purpose of experimenting. There is no need to concern yourselves as to the nature of his researches. The plain fact of the matter – as you have heard from Professor Burney – is that he drowned in a vat of...' he looked down at his notes, 'of fermenting wort. You have merely to address yourselves to determining whether his death was accidental, or was brought about by some outside agency. In doing so, you must have regard to the fact that Dawson was habituated to the carrying out of these experiments. Now, it might be that familiarity had bred contempt; that he was careless in placing the ladder. Hence, when he stretched out over the vat, to obtain a sample from a particular part of its surface, the ladder slipped. On that analysis it would, I think, be necessary to assume that the wound below the right ear was caused by contact with the rim of the vat. You then have to take regard of the fact that only his feet were protruding from the vat. You will have to decide whether that sequence of events is not only possible, but probable. If that is your conclusion, a verdict of accidental death would follow.'

The coroner paused, and looked challengingly round the court. 'Alternatively,' he went on, 'you must consider whether his death was brought about by the intervention of another person. I must emphasise that no evidence has been led as to the presence of any other person at the scene. But you would be entitled to assume that in a brewery, where processes are carried out continuously, other men would be on the premises. In pursuing that theory, you could assume that his putative assailant either mounted the ladder behind him, or another ladder. In either case, the deceased would be aware of the presence of his assailant... There is yet another possibility. An attack could have been made upon the deceased while both he and his attacker were on terra firma. This would entail the assumption that the assailant rendered him unconscious with a blow to the head, carried his inert body up a ladder, and tossed him into the vat to drown. You will have to weigh the likelihood of this sequence of events. If you conclude that, on the evidence, the probability is that Professor Dawson met his death through the intervention of another person, you should return a verdict of unlawful killing by person or persons unknown... You may now retire.'

Sir Rufus stood, bowed and stalked out of the courtroom. There was a murmur of conversation; the jurors filed out of the court; Farnaby sidled sheepishly away.

'Come to watch the Roman circus?' It was Lubbock behind them.

'It's our job,' Bragg said gruffly.

'Mine too! We don't want anybody saying Tyrrell's were at fault.'

'You must be pleased with this morning, then.'

Lubbock scowled. 'I was none too pleased at the implication that one of our workers could have dotted him one. Or that silly sod Turnbury saying our water could be contaminated.'

'You will live it down... By the way,' Bragg went on straightfaced, 'we shall be expecting you to drain that vat for us.'

'What the hell are you talking about?'

'Well, sir, you remember Turnbury explaining Dawson's method – the bit about filling little bottles from the vat?'

'Yes.'

'If somebody bludgeoned him while he was leaning over collecting samples, like as not he would let go of his little bottle. Now, if we don't find a bottle in there, it could be he was killed elsewhere and dumped on you.'

'Don't be bloody stupid!' Lubbock exclaimed. 'How would anyone smuggle a corpse into our brewery?'

'You have carts going in and out all the time.'

'Well, you are welcome to sort through the bottom of the vat, if you want. It was pumped out this morning. You would enjoy that... I'll tell you what! You two clean it out, and I'll see you get the customary pint for your trouble!'

Bragg and Morton lunched on pork pie and strong tea at a cafe, then made their way back to the coroner's court. They found Hunt standing by the door.

'Come back for the second act, have you?' Bragg remarked.

'I had to give a lecture... What has been happening?'

184

'Oh, we had the usual knockabout stuff. After Farnaby on insurance and your Hunt on Thermodynamics, we had Turnbury on Turnbury. Then, to top the bill, Burney on bodies. Quite a good day so far... By the way, have you found anyone who saw you at Lord's yet?'

'I will... Speaking of Turnbury, there is staff-room gossip that he is intimate with Rosalie Dawson.'

'What, knocking her off?'

'If, by that expression, you mean are they lovers, the answer would appear to be yes.'

'He's nothing but a lad – still in his twenties... But she might like a bit of variety. Hello! They are going in.'

They had barely taken their places, before they had to stand for the coroner to make his entrance. Sir Rufus looked anything but amiable. As he took his seat the jury began to file back into court. Their expressions varied from resentment to defiance.

Sir Rufus raised his head. 'Will the foreman please stand,' he said truculently. 'I understand that the jury is having difficulty in arriving at a verdict.'

The foreman bowed his head. 'That is the case, your honour.'

'You are mumbling, man! The whole court must hear you – to the back of the public gallery. It is the immutable requirement of justice – that it must be public.'

'We are evenly split, your honour,' the foreman said loudly.

'I see ... Is there any point of law on which you desire instruction?'

'No, sir.'

'Then, what is preventing you from reaching at least a majority verdict?'

The foreman took a deep breath. 'We are apprised of the fact that the deceased has been doing this research at Tyrrell's brewery, over a long period. From what we are told, he carried out the same procedures every time he went there – taking samples, putting them in little bottles and labelling them. We accept the possibility that the ladder could slip sideways accidentally. Some of us are prepared to believe that this indeed happened. But as many of us ask why it should have happened on this occasion, without external intervention.'

'Is there is no possibility of resolving this conflict?'

'None, your honour. The two parties are entrenched in their opinions.'

Sir Rufus frowned. 'Then, your only course is to return an open verdict,' he said coldly.

'Very well, sir. Then we so do.'

The coroner glared at him, then got to his feet and strode angrily from the court.

'I think we will keep out of his way for a bit,' Bragg said gruffly. 'I don't fancy playing the part of an Aunt Sally!'

Fanny Hildred dismissed the hansom at the top of Tan House Lane. She began to walk down the street with some trepidation. Not that the houses were overbearing; they were ordinary workers' terraces, built perhaps seventy years ago. But the pallid London clay bricks were now soot-blackened, giving the walls a menacing solidity. Fanny felt panic rising in her. When she had planned this visit, it seemed a perfectly justifiable, utterly normal act. She had shrugged off the uncomfortable fact, that she knew perfectly well Mr Bragg would not be at home. She would be no more than an acquaintance happening to be in the area, and making a chance call. The kind of thing that happened all the time... She switched her thoughts to a happier channel. Mr Bragg must come up this street every morning. He would walk, of course, swinging along purposefully, solidly. Off to a day of upholding the law, tracking down malefactors; then walking in the evening sun back home... Back to Mrs Jenks...

Mr Bragg had spoken occasionally of his dead wife. In his memory of her there seemed to be a tenderness, a lingering regret for what might have been. But Fanny did not believe that he still mourned her. It was all too long ago... Yet, if that were true, why had he not remarried? She had become haunted by the suspicion that there was no need to; that the relationship between him and Mrs Jenks was closer than that between landlady and lodger. After all, it was the staple of seaside marionette shows, of music hall comedians. Roger the lodger... She smiled at her imaginings. One could not think of anyone less like a Lothario than Mr Bragg!... Yet she was sure that the growing friendship between them had a physical dimension. The way he looked at her, sought her company; seemed to take her hand on the slightest pretext. And yet, he seemed to back away before any explicit intimacy could arise. She had told herself that his innate sense of respect, of decency, prevented any advances. This had given her hope. On the right occasion, in the right situation, he might be brought to the point... Over the last few days they had become much closer; sitting in the theatre together, walking arm-in-arm through the park, eating late suppers in basement cafes and laughing together! Despite his grim and responsible work, there was a well of fun – of happiness inside him. On his visits to Dorset she had sensed it. But it had always been overlaid by a ridiculous deference. Here, in London, in his own milieu, he had been freer, more confident, less concerned with convention. It had been exciting; she had glimpsed a better future than moulder-ing away in Bere Regis. She had begun building castles in the air...

So she must know! Men were deceivers ever, or so the song claimed. Her life as a single woman, in a small Dorset village, was unstimulating; indeed, downright dull. But it was worthy... To her newly critical mind, the very phrase sounded like a condemnation. But suppose her hopes were dashed?... Well, if they were, she could always fall back on being worthy. She smiled at this moral inversion. Perhaps, some day, she would be able to tell Joseph Bragg of the day when she chose between virtue and a relationship with him!

She paused outside number eleven. She had written the address a score of times without ever trying to visualise the house. It was of two storeys, at the end of a terrace. It seemed to possess a cellar also. She peered through a paling fence. That must be the garden which gave Mr Bragg so much pleasure. He spoke of it as if it were his own ... which, of course, it was, since he tended it. Whatever the relationship between him and Mrs Jenks, it was his home... She screwed up her courage, mounted the steps and knocked on the door. She had a moment of panic as she heard footsteps within. A key turned in the lock and the door swung open.

'Yes?'

She was in her forties, and grey-haired. She was wearing a white blouse, pinned at the collar with a jet brooch. Over her full black skirt she had on a flowered apron ... she looked reassuringly old-fashioned.

'Mrs Jenks?'

'Yes.'

'My name is Fanny Hildred, from Dorset. We are friends of Mr Bragg...'

'Oh, yes. I've heard of you.'

'I half expected to find him here.'

'No. He is at work.'

'Oh, dear! What a pity. And he has told us so much about you and his life here. I had hoped to be able to see where he lives, so that I can visualise what he is referring to in his letters.'

Mrs Jenks frowned. 'Well, you can come in, if that's what you want. I don't suppose it would matter to him either way.'

Fanny followed her in. At least Mrs Jenks

was decidedly plain.

'His rooms are upstairs,' Mrs Jenks said. 'I won't come up with you. I don't go up more than I have to, because of my knees.'

Fanny smiled. 'I will not disturb anything, I promise you,' she said.

There were two rooms on the upper floor. At the front was a sitting-room with a small cast-iron fireplace. There was a gate-leg table on the opposite wall, and a bookcase under the window. A small bureau was on one side of the fireplace and a comfortable chair on the other. Fanny smiled to herself as she saw an ashtray with a pipe in it, on the bookcase. It was pleasantly homely. In the bedroom was an iron-framed single bed, a wash-stand and a chest of drawers. A cupboard had been constructed on one side of the fireplace. She carefully eased open the door. It was crammed with coats and trousers, hung up carelessly. She suddenly had a pang of pity, of remorse. This was the converse of the capable, self-assured man who had been squiring her around. Here was someone who had suffered at the hands of fate, whose self-esteem had been eroded, who sometimes did not care...

She went downstairs again. Mrs Jenks was waiting for her in the hallway.

'Thank you so much, Mrs Jenks,' she said. 'When I read his letters, I shall be able to visualise everything he is referring to. And I am pleased to have met you.'

Mrs Jenks smiled. 'I'll tell him you came, miss,' she said. 'He'll be surprised, I should think.'

'No! I would much prefer it if you did not,' Fanny said firmly. 'I would like to tell him, myself, when the time is ripe.'

'And when will that be, miss?'

Fanny smiled. 'It could be sooner than any of us thinks,' she said.

Bragg tapped at the Commissioner's door, half hoping that he would be out.

'Come!'

He went in. Sir William looked up, gestured to a chair and went on reading. Eventually he tossed the report into his out-tray.

'Hardly an operational success, was it?' he asked petulantly. 'I had the chairman of the watch committee in, not an hour ago. Dear God! An open verdict...'

'The coroner wasn't too pleased either, sir,' Bragg said.

'But that is not the point! It reflects on the police. People will be asking why more has not been done to bring those responsible to justice!'

'That is a bit unfair, sir,' Bragg said mildly. 'There is an outside chance that it was an accident. You don't believe it, neither do I. But to most of the people in that court-room, any suggestion that Dawson had been murdered would be a surprise. What does the watch committee know that we don't?'

'I doubt if they know half as much,' the Commissioner said. 'But they will use any stick to belabour us.'

'Well, at least an open verdict gives us room to pursue the matter without raising hackles,' Bragg said. 'And there are a few leads.'

'Such as?'

Bragg leaned back in his chair. 'I suppose we could say that there are three groups of Dawson.'

'Three groups?'

'Yes, sir. Only five suspects in all, but among them there would be three different motives.'

'Well. Go on, man!'

'You have to understand, sir, that Dawson was very fond of the ladies. And he seems to have got his way with a couple in addition to his wife. The first, believe it or not, was a vicar's wife.'

'A what?'

'Mrs Jennifer Calder, the wife of the vicar of St Mark's, Whitefriars. I don't know what they get up to at Tyrrell's Christmas parties, but Dawson picked up a couple of women there... As I say, Mrs Calder was one of them. She must have been easy pickings, for someone like Dawson. Her husband had been a padre with the army in South Africa. Apparently he was badly wounded, by a mortar bomb, at the battle of Majuba Hill. As his wife delicately put it, it left him less than a man. Mrs Calder seems to be an ordinary, warm-natured woman, just the mark for our friend Dawson.'

'Are you saying that she was his mistress?'

the Commissioner asked aghast. 'That she would betray a wounded member of our forces?'

'That's right, sir. They used to go to a hotel in King's Cross for their little romps.'

'Great heavens! How sordid!'

'Yes. But she reckoned Calder should never have married her. So she was justified.'

'I cannot believe it!'

'I can, sir. After chatting with the Rev. Calder, I reckon he ought to be locked up in a lunatic asylum, not running a parish... He is certainly unbalanced enough to commit murder, and think he was perfectly justified.'

The Commissioner cleared his throat. 'Nevertheless,' he said, 'it is a situation that must be handled with utmost delicacy. Please refer to me, before making any move to arrest him. Do you understand?'

'Yes, sir,' Bragg said drily. 'You will probably feel the same about the second of our cuckolds.'

'Who is he?'

'A man called John Eldridge. He is a lawyer.'

'I detest being involved with these top-hat criminals, Bragg,' Sir William complained.

'Yes, sir ... Dawson met Eldridge's wife, Caroline, at a Christmas party at Tyrrell's too. I don't know if it was the same one as when he tickled the fancy of Mrs Calder, or not. But I reckon Dawson was quite capable of keeping any number of women on the go at once!'

The Commissioner flushed with embarrassment. 'And what connection had she with Tyrrell's?' he asked.

'Her husband is the solicitor who acts for the brewery... He must have been at the party, when Dawson was giving her the chat.'

'I see ... yes. Certainly the arrest of a solicitor of the supreme court is not a thing to embark on lightly.'

'Then, I will refer to you, sir?'

'Yes... Unless, of course, operational necessity dictates more precipitate action. In which case, you, er...'

'Very good, sir... Now, you are going to like this next bit. For, while Dawson was going around stuffing other people's wives, his own was dropping her drawers for one of his students.'

'You have this on good authority?' Sir William asked.

'From a senior lecturer at University College, named Hunt. He told us at the inquest, so we have not yet followed it up.'

The Commissioner frowned. 'But it does not make sense!' he exclaimed. 'On the one hand you are saying that Dawson was excessively virile; on the other, that his wife was driven to, er, seek her amusement with a student.'

'Oh, it could happen,' Bragg assured him. 'Some women are as hot-blooded as any man. Such a one might well look out for a bit of variety, especially with a younger man. After all, a lad in his mid-twenties would be able to...'

'Yes, yes, Bragg,' Sir William interposed. 'I take your point... Therein might lie a motive for murder. But it is evident that the murderer must have had detailed knowledge of the brewery.'

'Ah, did I not say, sir? This lad is called Turnbury. He used to work at Tyrrell's, alongside Dawson... Come to think of it, he might have a motive beyond stuffing Dawson's wife. Turnbury has been researching in the very same field as Dawson – though no longer in the same brewery, I gather. It seems to me there could hardly be room for two authorities on coliform bacteria at the college. So that sounds like a powerful case for Turnbury as the murderer.'

'That is something of an improvement,' Sir William said. 'I must confess that a prosecution case, based solely on evidence of infidelity between the parties, does not fill me with confidence.'

'And we do have another suspect, whose morals might be purer than the others, if not his motives.'

'Good heavens! Another?'

'The senior lecturer, Hunt. He could be in line for the next professorship.'

The Commissioner gave a crafty smile. 'Pure ambition, then,' he said.

'Exactly, sir,' Bragg said, straight-faced. 'And, as it happens, he has recently designed some new plant for the brewery.

So clearly he knows his way around the place.'

'So he forms a group of one, with academic ambition as his motive, rather than carnal desires?'

'Well put, sir.'

'And, have you interviewed all the suspects?'

'Not yet. I have still to see a banker, name of Anscombe. His firm acts for Tyrrell's. Mrs Dawson says she was with him, the afternoon her husband died.'

'I see. And have you no firm evidence to charge any of them? I do not mind telling you, Bragg, I am under considerable pressure.'

Bragg tugged at his moustache thoughtfully. 'Well, sir,' he said. 'We could arrest them all. It's not as if we could be accused of picking up the first five people we came across. But, if it is a murder, I don't see more than one person being involved. So you would still be arresting four innocent people.'

'Hmm...' Sir William pondered. 'One thing I am clear about,' he said at length, 'there can be no question of arresting these people on mere suspicion. It would be far too... Continental. Yes. You will have to put some flesh on it, Bragg. And do not take long about it!'

6

Bragg and Morton were walking along Fleet Street in the warm sun. Being Saturday morning, some of the clerks had dispensed with their sober black attire. One or two of the younger men were even sporting striped blazers. There were also a few female clerks, swishing along in their black skirts and white blouses, pretending not to see the admiring glances of the men. It was the only good thing that had happened in his time, Bragg thought; replacing steel pens with typewriting machines. It had taken longer in the City than most other places. Tradition reigned supreme in the Square Mile. It was only because men couldn't get their fingers round the keyboard, that the women had been let in. Now he knew of nobody that regretted it. When he had started work in the shipping office, every letter had to be reproduced in a large copy-book. It could sometimes take an age to find what you were looking for. Now, with this new carbon-paper, they could keep all the correspondence with one customer in one file. Files a woman could lift easily. Soon there would be little need for male clerks in these offices. That might mean less crime, or at least less fraud...

'There is Gosling & Hoare's bank, sir,' Morton said.

'What?... Ah, yes. What's the betting Anscombe will have taken the morning off? I'm sure I would, if I owned a slice of this lot.'

They went through a pillared entrance porch, and into a great domed banking-hall. Opposite the doorway was a long mahogany counter, with divisions every four feet or so. Not many people coming here would want their business made public, Bragg thought. But, partitions or not, you would have to keep your voice down. He strode over to the counter and banged on a bell. After some moments, a fresh-faced young man came hurrying across. He looked at them reproachfully.

'Can I be of assistance to you, gentlemen?' he asked.

'City police,' Bragg said firmly. 'We want to see Mr Anscombe.'

The clerk looked disconcerted. 'Have you an appointment, sir?' he asked.

'We don't make appointments. Is he in?'

'Well ... yes, he is in attendance.'

'Then bloody well get him to attend to us!'

'I ... just a moment, sir.' He disappeared through a door behind the counter.

'I bet Anscombe is doing a runner,' Bragg said darkly.

Morton laughed. 'I doubt it. Even if he were implicated in some way, the City's style would be to brazen it out.'

'Yes ... to start thinking of the favours you could call in, to get you off the hook. Well, he had better not be long, that's all!'

They waited for almost ten minutes; Bragg had begun to prowl impatiently about. Then the young man returned.

'Would you please follow me,' he said.

He led them down a passage which seemed prosaic, after the flamboyance of the banking-hall. They were ushered into a large room, richly carpeted, with a crystal gasolier and heavy curtains. The man who rose from the desk, to greet them, was in his early forties, Bragg decided. His hair was grizzled, his forehead lined. He seemed entirely composed.

'You are police officers, I believe,' he said, holding out his hand.

'Yes, sir. Sergeant Bragg and Constable Morton, of the City police.'

Anscombe smiled. 'Not Jim Morton, the cricketer? Well, this is obviously going to be an auspicious day. I have been wanting to meet you for ages!' He shook Morton's hand warmly, then made to shake Bragg's also.

'This is not a social call,' Bragg said brusquely, disregarding the outstretched hand. 'We have some questions for you, relating to the death of Professor Edward Dawson.'

A wary look spread over Anscombe's face. 'I see ... I will, of course, help you in the matter, to the limited extent that I can.'

'Right.' Bragg drew up a chair to the desk, and waited till Anscombe was seated.

'First of all, sir, would you mind giving us your private address?'

'Certainly.' Anscombe paused until Morton had got out his pad and pencil. 'Twelve, Ridgmount Gardens – behind Gower Street. That is Ridgmount without an "e", officer.'

'And are you one of the principals of Gosling & Hoare's bank?'

'I am the only significant shareholder, sergeant. A fact which gives me some comfort, in the present climate.'

'Meaning?'

'Oh, commercial life is changing at a fearful rate. Trade is becoming ever more frenetic and unpredictable. The old certainties have gone.'

'I expect every generation has said that, sir.'

Anscombe frowned. 'No doubt,' he said. 'But in the old days there were clear demarcations. Everyone knew their place, as it were. But now, every business seems intent on expanding, regardless of the fact that there is a finite number of customers. Our clients are clamouring for extended credit – clients who, in this modern context, all too often prove not to be credit-worthy... In my father's day all our clients were gentlemen, whose word was their bond. Nowadays, I regret to say, the term gentleman means precious little any more. Indeed, were it not for our considerable connection with the landed gentry, Gosling & Hoare would be in a parlous state.'

'Well, we are not here to talk about your business, sir, but about you.'

Anscombe smiled confidently. 'Then, fire away!' he said.

'When were you aware of the death of Professor Dawson?'

Anscombe's eyes narrowed. 'I have just read the report of the inquest, in this morning's *City Press*,' he said carefully.

'Did you know him?'

'Only by common report.'

Bragg smiled. 'I would not exactly call Rosalie Dawson common,' he said. 'Her morals a bit loose by most people's standards, but choosy with it.'

Anscombe remained silent, but watchful.

'She says, sir, that you and she are lovers.'

'Ah! And now Edward Dawson is dead, eh?'

'That's right, sir... Are you married, yourself?'

Anscombe looked out of the window for a moment, then he swung back. 'I see no reason whatever, why I should not cooperate fully in your enquiries, sergeant... Yes, I was married. My wife died four years ago, it was unexpected, and the loss had a great impact on me. I became morose and unsociable. I even contemplated suicide. In a sense, someone else's tragedy became my salvation. Our senior partner – for no doubt the best of reasons – invested clients' money in speculative ventures. There was a downturn in trade, and many of those ventures failed... I was partly at fault, in not foreseeing the outcome. But John Gosling took the blame on his own shoulders.'

'Am I right in thinking that he shot himself?' Bragg asked.

'That is correct. As a result, I was catapulted into the distinctly uncomfortable position of senior partner. But, at least, I could give the matter my whole and undivided attention. I am relieved to say that we have now turned the corner.'

'So you have time for a bit of the old rumpy-tumpy?'

Anscombe did not reply.

'How did you come to meet Rosalie Dawson, sir?'

Anscombe gave a tentative smile. 'It was at a reception in Tyrrell's brewery, to mark Christmas... I think, two years ago. George Tyrrell had invited her with her husband. He could not come, but, to my great good fortune, she decided to attend. We were introduced, and had a pleasant conversation. We have many interests in common... I suppose it could well have ended there. But, a month or so later, she made an appointment to see me at the bank. You must understand that Rosalie comes from a very wealthy family. And, although we did not act for her father, we could not have advised him better. When he died he left the bulk of his fortune in separate trusts for his three daughters. The trustees are professional men of impeccable reputation and integrity.'

'So Dawson could not get his hands on the money?'

'No. I gather that he made an attempt to get himself appointed a trustee of his wife's trust. He had a kind of arrogance, which often goes with intellectual distinction. In addition, certain infidelities were reported; so the trustees resisted his proposal.'

'Good for them! But why did she really come to see you? After all, Gosling & Hoare are no safer, no better at investing than a score of other concerns.'

Anscombe smiled. 'I asked myself the same question, sergeant. And I found none of the answers repugnant. So far as our present purposes are concerned, we agreed to act on behalf of Rosalie's trustees.'

'Ah, but our present purposes go far beyond banking.' Bragg said sternly. 'Bank accounts don't kill people.'

'Agreed... Of course, Rosalie had certain monies outside the trust fund. She suggested that we should meet – take tea at the Savoy – so that I could confer with her on investment strategy. This became a weekly event – a purely social occasion.'

'I see ... and how long did it stay pure?' Bragg asked roughly.

'To us it has always been so. However our mutual affection grew rapidly ... I was living in a large, family house in Surrey I and seven servants. It was patently absurd, but it had been my marital home. I suppose that Ros gave me the impetus to reshape my life. I sold the house, and took a lease on my Ridgmount Gardens apartment. She advised me on furnishings, and so on; this entailed frequent meetings there. Not surprisingly, we became lovers.'

'Hmm... And when was this?'

'Two years ago. In the summer of '93. We would meet on most Wednesdays there.'

'And were you content with that?'

Anscombe shrugged. 'Not content, no. But there was nothing we could do. In the present state of the law, a wife cannot divorce her husband, unless she can prove that he has been carrying on an incestuous relationship. Rosalie could make no such allegation.'

'Did you not ask Dawson to divorce her?'

Anscombe's eyes widened. 'Of course not!

She would have had to live with the public stigma.'

'I see. As usual women want it every way... And, are you saying that Dawson did not know his wife was having it off with you?'

Anscombe flinched. 'That is unnecessarily pejorative!' he said.

'I see. You are different from other people, are you? Yours was a pure, unsullied friendship, was it? Next, you will be telling me you were with the Archbishop of Canterbury, at the time Dawson was killed!' He paused, then: 'Where were you on the afternoon of Saturday the twenty-second of June?' he asked formally.

'I was with Rosalie, shopping in the West End.'

'Hmm... Very convenient, that. So you can give each other an alibi?'

'Naturally.'

'And is there anyone else who can vouch for you?'

Anscombe shook his head. 'I think that is highly improbable, sergeant.'

After lunch in a pub, Bragg and Morton

walked towards Bedford Square.

'By the way, sir,' Morton said. 'I was glancing through Dawson's desk diary last night. At the beginning of June – Friday the seventh, in fact – there was an entry that I found both surprising and perhaps significant.'

'Go on, lad. Astonish me!'

'Most of the diary is in a kind of code. But, on that day, he had scribbled a pencil entry. This was to the effect that he had tried to replicate Turnbury's research results, and failed. He added the comment: "Fabricated?"'

'Bloody hell! Was it true, do you think? I mean, can we take it at face value?'

'They both worked in the same field. So Dawson was well qualified to rework Turnbury's experiments.'

'But why would he bother?'

Morton shrugged. 'Perhaps to safeguard his own position. It is a fact that Dawson supervised Turnbury's research. He told us so himself. There must have been some antagonism between them. If you remember, Turnbury said that Dawson's main interest was in advancing his own reputation. But the animosity could have had other roots.'

'You mean, Turnbury's extra-curricular activities with Mrs Dawson?'

'Indeed! Because a man is unfaithful himself, it does not mean that he would tolerate adultery in his wife. It could well have prompted a desire to cast doubt on Turnbury's academic ability.'

'Hmm... If it were true, he could have felt it was his clear duty.' Bragg tugged at his ragged moustache. 'Friday the seventh, eh?'

'Yes, sir. Just over two weeks before Dawson was murdered.'

'So why did our killer wait so long?'

Morton frowned. 'Dawson might not have confronted Turnbury immediately. Indeed, it is possible that he did not confront him at all. Dawson might have been devious enough to tell his wife of the discovery, knowing full well that it would get back to Turnbury.'

'Hmm... Yes. That would take him down a peg or two in Mrs Dawson's eyes. But Turnbury cannot have thought he could

215

keep it quiet, can he? Why wait a fortnight, if he intends to kill him?'

'Presumably he has to wait for an opportunity; for when Dawson is in the old vat house alone.'

'But we do not have any mention of Turnbury in the brewery that day,' Bragg objected.

'Nor of anyone else, other than a phantom maiden and employees of the brewery.'

'And we assume that none of them would have a motive. Are we assuming that too readily?'

Morton shrugged. 'It is possible,' he said.

'Well, here we are; the residence of the victim. I wonder if he knew Anscombe lived so close.'

Bragg rang the bell and stepped back. The bow of black crape had vanished from the knocker, the curtains were pulled back, there were flowers in the window. Life had to go on, true. But this seemed indecent.

The door was opened by the maid.

'Good afternoon, Mildred,' Bragg said cheerfully. 'City police. We would like to see Mrs Dawson.'

The girl looked doubtful. 'Wait there,' she said, and half closed the door.

'A policeman's lot is, indeed, not a happy one,' Morton said with a grin.

They waited for some minutes, Bragg becoming increasingly restive, then the maid reappeared. She escorted them to the sitting-room overlooking the square. Mrs Dawson was sitting by the fireplace. She was dressed in black, and had a square of black silk over her hair. She rose as they entered.

Bragg took her hand. 'May I say how much we admired your self-possession at the funeral, ma'am,' he said warmly. 'Most women would have broken down, it being so sudden.'

Mrs Dawson managed a wry smile. 'It was numbness, rather than self-possession,' she said. 'I am only now facing up to the enormity of my loss.'

'Yes, of course. Tell me, ma'am, did your husband ever talk to you about the work he did?'

'No, officer. Such qualities as I have do not embrace the scientific.'

'We are probably worse off than you are, ma'am.'

'Then I suggest that you approach his admiring students.'

'Such as Turnbury, you mean? We have already had a chat with him. He told us how your late husband set about taking samples from the vat at Tyrrell's. We are not clear whether he was interested in the type of bacteria, or their concentration, or both. We wondered if you had any notes of his, that might help us.'

Mrs Dawson frowned. 'I doubt it,' she said. 'He was – dare I say it – somewhat neurotic about his work. Students often had to wait in his college room for him – sometimes for protracted periods. So he made his notes in a kind of personal shorthand, to prevent his discoveries being purloined.'

'I see,' Bragg said comfortingly. 'So we would not have understood them anyway... You were not at the inquest, of course.'

'No, officer. I instructed our ... my solicitor to attend, as you suggested. I understand that the jury returned an open verdict.'

'Yes, ma'am. The coroner was not best pleased. But if he wanted a murder verdict, he should have made it clearer for the jury.'

'Murder?' she said, aghast.

'Oh, yes. According to the pathologist, the signs could hardly be clearer.'

She dabbed at her eyes with a black-bordered handkerchief.

'Poor Edward,' she said. 'He was always so sure that he was in control of everything.'

'I expect he was, as long as everybody behaved within the rules of polite society. But somebody was pushed that little bit too far.'

'Pushed?'

'And, in his turn, that was literally what happened to your husband. He must have been up his ladder, when somebody got up behind him, hit him over the head with a piece of timber, and shoved him into the vat. The trouble, for us, is that there are scores of people scurrying about at Tyrrell's, any one of whom could have done it. And that leaves out of the reckoning people who have been invited to parties, and such, on the premises. So we are having to concentrate on motives, on finding the people who wanted him dead.'

Mrs Dawson winced. 'I cannot think there are any such,' she said.

'Oh, I don't know about that... What about Anscombe, for instance? He is the effective owner of Gosling & Hoare, who are bankers to Tyrrell's. He, like you and a score of others, has been to the brewery for parties and the like; been shown round the premises. He would have wanted your husband dead, because he wants to marry you. He admitted as much.'

'Poor Charles!' Her smile held a touch of pity. 'He is a good friend, and has been supportive and caring over these dreadful days. But I never encouraged him to think that our relationship could become really close.'

'So what is going to bed with a man supposed to suggest to him?' Bragg asked brusquely.

She gave him a wounded look. 'Apparently that he can make free with my confidences.'

'I see. I have never met a woman who

could copulate in confidence before,' Bragg said brutally. 'Where were you at the time of your husband's death, anyway?'

Her face was white, she stared uncomprehendingly at him.

'Where were you on the afternoon of the twenty-second of June?'

'This ... this is no way to treat a lady,' she wailed.

'In my book there are no ladies, only women; some luckier than others, but none above the law.'

She dropped her head. 'I was in the West End, shopping.'

'Who with?'

'Charles Anscombe.'

'Very convenient!' Bragg said roughly. 'If I were advising either of you, I would suggest you find an unimpeachable witness, who would stand up in court to swear to that. The Pope might just about fill the bill.'

From Bedford Square Bragg and Morton strolled to University College. They found Waller in the library, and beckoned him into the corridor.

'We seem to be going round and round, chasing our own tail, over this Dawson business,' Bragg said confidingly. 'I wonder if you can give us a bit more help.'

Waller shrugged. 'You do me too much honour,' he said. 'I am only half-way up my own particular tree.'

'But you know, better than most, what Dawson was up to... Now, we have talked to goodness knows how many people, and the name Pasteur keeps cropping up – particularly in regard to brewing.'

'That is hardly surprising,' Waller said. 'He must be one of the truly great men of science. Without his discoveries, we could still be a nation of village economies – so far as perishable foodstuffs are concerned, anyway.'

'Really?'

'Well, perhaps that overstates it somewhat. But, in the seventies, Pasteur made crucial discoveries concerning bacteria. He developed the modern microscope. This technique enabled him to study entities invisible to the naked eyes. His experiments – partly conducted at Whitbread's brewery, here in the City – led to the adoption of pasteurism in the most forward-looking breweries.'

'What is pasteurism?' Bragg asked.

'It is a process which destroys bacteria in the wort. It involves maintaining a temperature of one hundred and forty degrees Fahrenheit, for around half an hour after fermentation. It does not totally remove the possibility of infection, but it reduces it very considerably. One might almost say that Pasteur made the large-scale production of beer a commercial possibility.'

'And, do Tyrrell's practise pasteurism?'

'No. That is why Dawson could still experiment there.'

'I see. Right. Now, you followed Turnbury as Dawson's assistant.'

'Hardly assistant,' Waller said sharply.

'Yes, I know ... he was your supervisor. By the way, we gather that Turnbury is working in the professor's field – wort-spoiling bacteria.'

'That is correct.'

'What stage has Turnbury reached now?'

'You mean, on the academic ladder?'

'Yes.'

'He has already received his M.Sc. degree. He has been appointed a junior lecturer, and has begun to work towards his doctorate of philosophy.'

'Philosophy? I can't see much philosophy in studying bugs you can't even see!'

Waller shrugged. 'One becomes philosophical at one's inability to keep up with their evolution, I imagine.'

'Hmm... What kind of man is Turnbury?'

'I cannot claim to know him well. One has but little interaction with one's predecessors.'

'Even if you are more or less working in the same field, like wort-spoilers?'

'Research, sergeant, at least in the UCL science department, is not a co-operative venture.'

'Hmm.' Bragg paused, then: 'What was it like, working with Dawson?' he asked.

Waller snorted. 'Do you mean, was it a privilege?' he asked.

'If you like.'

'In one sense, it was – if not a privilege,

then an enlightening experience. In the firmament of science, Dawson was a star of at least the second magnitude.'

Bragg grunted. 'It sounds as if you have worked hard at polishing that one,' he said. 'And yet most people, including his wife, seem to think that he was a bit of a pig.'

Waller smiled. 'I could hardly comment on his marital relationship,' he said. 'I have enough difficulty in keeping my own intended happy.'

'Ah. And who is she?'

'Lily Simkins; the daughter of the house where I lodge.'

'You will be aiming to get married, then?'

'That would be impossible, while I am a student.'

'How long to go?'

'Two years to my Master's degree. Then it would depend on how soon I could get a reasonable job.'

'And how old is Miss Simkins?'

'Almost twenty-one.'

'No wonder she gets ratty with you! So, Turnbury is a junior lecturer. Is that a permanent post?'

'No. It helps the authorities to assess the incumbent's potential.'

'And?'

'Anyone without real ability would be quietly got rid of.'

'So you believe you have the needful?'

'I do. Whether other people share my judgement, I shall discover in due course!'

'Hmm... So Turnbury could find himself without a job, could he?'

'Indeed.'

'And who would wield the chopper? People like Dawson?'

Waller shrugged. 'I have no doubt that, in the event, he would have been consulted.'

'But not any more...'

'One has to accept that a probationary period is not unreasonable,' Waller went on. 'As I may find to my cost. A great number of students can be harmed by one un-inspiring lecturer, during the course of his career.'

'Could Dawson inspire people?'

'I would not be ploughing this lonely furrow, if he could not.'

'Huh! Is that your poetic soul, or you

practising being a lecturer?'

'A poetic soul would be an unnecessary piece of baggage in a scientist!'

'So, how did Dawson and Turnbury get on?'

Waller hesitated, looking down at his hands. 'Not always well,' he said reluctantly. 'Both of them are somewhat opinionated. It is rumoured that they had a fierce argument in the library, the other day. *Sotto voce*, but intense.'

'What about?'

'No one knows.'

'I see.' Bragg sighed. 'I don't mind admitting that we are in difficulty in this case, sir. Policemen are very ordinary people. I left school myself at nine. So what you are talking about is way over my head. Now, what I would like, is for you to come with us to Tyrrell's, and show us exactly what Dawson was doing.'

Waller demurred. 'I am really rather busy,' he said.

'But I am sure you would not set your private affairs above the catching of a dangerous criminal,' Bragg said unctuously.

'That would seem to give me little choice... Very well.'

They found a growler outside the college gates, and directed the driver to take them to Tyrrell's brewery. Once there, Bragg held back, and let Waller lead them towards the old vat house. One or two workmen nodded to him as they passed. As they neared the building, Lubbock came hurrying up.

'I have a present for you,' he remarked. 'Don't say we are not doing our best to help.' He dropped a small glass bottle into Bragg's palm.

'From the small vat?'

'Right. We couldn't wait any longer for you and the constable to clean it out! Don't ever say we are not good citizens!... There is a new lot of wort in it now.' He walked away smiling to himself.

Bragg showed it to Waller. 'Would this be the bottle Dawson was holding when he drowned?' he asked.

'It is certainly the type of bottle he used, to take samples.'

Bragg frowned. 'I can never get a straight answer from you,' he grumbled.

'That is because your questions are insufficiently precise. It is possible that Dawson was holding this bottle. One might say that, since only he and I are experimenting here, at the moment, and since I have certainly not dropped a bottle in the vat, your proposition is probable. But no more than that. After all, Dawson came here frequently. He could have dropped it on a previous occasion.'

Morton expected an explosion of wrath, but Bragg contented himself with a quiet 'Very well, sir... Now, would you set the ladder where Dawson would have put it when taking samples?'

Waller went across to the longer of the two ladders, and propped it against the side of the small vat.

'Is that the angle it would have been at?' Bragg asked. 'Let's assume he was taking samples from the middle.'

Waller pulled the foot of the ladder out. 'Then, it would have been more like that,' he said.

'Yes... To tell you the truth, sir, it's a bit hard for a plodding copper, like me, to visualise. Would you mind going up, and show us what he would have been doing? Here is his little bottle.'

Waller took it from him impatiently. 'Very well,' he said.

Bragg got hold of the ladder, to steady it as Waller climbed upwards. He had reached the rim of the vat now, and was going still higher... He had the glass bottle in his right hand, holding on to the ladder with his left. He leaned out to his right, the bottle just touching the surface of the liquid. Bragg took his hands off the ladder... It was still stable. In a moment the bottle would be full. Bragg seized the ladder and twisted it violently. There was a cry, and Waller disappeared into the vat.

'Quick, lad,' Bragg said with a grin, 'get him out. We don't want another inquest!'

Morton mounted the ladder and helped the sodden Waller out of the vat.

Bragg pressed a half-crown into his hand. 'It was my fault, for not holding tightly enough,' he said. 'This should cover the cost of getting your clothes cleaned.'

Waller took the coin angrily, and

squelched out of the vat house.

'Cocky little bastard!' Bragg said. 'Anyway, we can see how it might have happened ... I tell you what! That was the best halfcrown I have spent in many a long day!'

'Yes,' Morton remarked. 'And he fell into the middle of the vat. No feet sticking out. That would seem to suggest that Dawson was using the smaller of the two ladders.'

'Hmm... The question is, who was around to see that he drowned?'

Bragg was strolling with Fanny, next day, over the lush grass of Green Park. They had walked around Buckingham Palace Gardens, Fanny expressing surprise and delight at every turn. But was it affected? Bragg wondered. She was a mature woman, if the truth were told. Perhaps the Sunday afternoon crowds were animating her. Certainly the Londoners were intent on enjoying themselves. Lollipop men were selling their wares at the very gates of the palace itself. And why not?... Fanny broke away to retrieve a ball, and throw it back to a child. Her face was glowing with pleasure as she took Bragg's arm again.

'I am so enjoying my stay here!' she said, looking up into his face. 'I would live just here, given half a chance!'

'You would need a king's ransom, miss,' Bragg said.

'But London is so stimulating! I love the bustle, the vigour, the sheer determination of people to enjoy themselves. The country is so predictable; every day like every other. And the shopping here! The prices are high, I grant you; but the choice!... It is a revelation after sleepy little Dorchester.'

'It's strange,' Bragg said, 'how people in the country want to live in the town, and townspeople want to live in the country.'

Fanny squeezed his arm. 'We are perverse and dissatisfied creatures, all of us!'

'Maybe. But I think that, at bottom, we all want to get back to our roots.'

'And, for you, that is Dorset ... I am glad to feel that we have so much in common.'

'But we are miles apart in class,' Bragg said.

'Perhaps... Yet here, in London, it does not

seem to matter.'

'In Dorset it would. Way back, my family were only tenant farmers.'

Fanny smiled. 'Then they probably grew barley; that my family turned into beer.'

'That my family duly drank!'

'You see! Mutual dependence – a heart-warming thought.'

'Yes... But soon I shall have to be making decisions. I have only one year left to serve in the police. Do I stay in London? Or do I find somewhere in the country to end my days?'

'From what you say, the choice is easy.'

Bragg frowned. 'Yes... But, you see, there is Mrs Jenks to consider. I have lived there for nearly twenty years; since before her husband died. Not that he was keen on having a copper as a lodger. He was a dustman, in a good way of business.'

'A dustman?' Fanny said, disdain in her voice.

'Yes. But he owned his own horse and cart. He was not best pleased when his wife decided to take a lodger – and a policeman at that! Still, we became good friends. We used to go to the pub on a Saturday night, for a pint and some jellied eels. We had some good times... Then Tommy cut his hand on a tin can. He shrugged it off. He'd cut himself scores of times, he said. But this time it took bad ways. Septicaemia, they said. Next minute he was a goner! So, for Mrs Jenks's sake, I stayed on. She needed the money.'

'I suppose that, in her turn, she might have stayed because she thought you needed a home.'

'Maybe. Life is complicated, isn't it?'

'But it need not be... Should you not sound her out? Find out what her intentions are?'

'Oh, I know them. She says she is going to live with her sister, in Southend.'

'Then your concern is needless... And here we are at the hotel. Will you come up to our suite, for tea?'

Bragg hesitated.

'Mamma will be there!' Fanny said. 'It will be perfectly proper.'

'All right. Just for a few minutes.'

The lift-boy whisked them up to the top

floor. Bragg took a childish delight in it. He would do the job for nothing, he thought; for the pure pleasure of soaring and plunging at the press of a lever. When they entered the room, Amy Hildred was seated on a sofa, surrounded by pieces of paper.

'Are the negotiations going well, ma'am?' Bragg asked.

Amy gathered her papers into a bundle. 'They must be nearing their end,' she said irritably. 'As to whether that will be good or bad, is still unsure.'

'Are Tyrrell's putting the squeeze on you, ma'am?'

'I have a minimum figure in my mind, Mr Bragg. They are creeping up towards that figure. If they do not agree to it, at our next meeting, then I shall keep the brewery. For the sake of my husband's memory, I will not sell it for less than it is worth.'

'I should think not!... I wonder, ma'am, if you can explain something to me. It's to do with the drowning at Tyrrell's.'

'I will try.'

'The technicalities of brewing are beyond me, and I am up against a lot of clever clogs,

235

who can run rings round me.'

Amy smiled. 'If I can understand it, Mr Bragg, I am sure that you can.'

'It is to do with fermenting. There was some discussion in the company, about switching from top-fermenting to bottom-fermenting. The professor who was killed had advocated the switch – which means I have got to try to understand it.'

Amy cocked her head. 'It is not difficult, so long as you do not get involved in the technicalities,' she said. 'Fundamentally, it is a question of what yeasts you use. Traditionally, English brewers have used top-fermenting yeasts.'

'Where do they get them from?' Bragg asked.

'Oh, each brewery will have its own strain. It grows, as you no doubt know by now.'

'We were looking at a vat yesterday. The fermentation had only just started, but we could see whitish knobs on the surface – a bit like cauliflowers.'

'That is the yeast. As fermentation progresses, the head grows until it blankets the vat. The brewer will use part of the head from one vat to start the fermentation in the next. And there is ample left over to sell to bakeries and so on.'

'So, what is wrong with that?'

'Nothing. Except that, if your strain of yeast becomes contaminated – infected by bacteria – you are transferring that infection to the new brew.'

'And, is the bottom-fermenting method better? If it is, I cannot see what the argument is all about.'

Amy smiled. 'I cannot pretend to know the technicalities,' she said. 'They are way above my head. I do know that the Germans use bottom fermentation. I take it that they use strains of yeast suited to that method. I know that they grow the yeasts they use in a laboratory. Also, they do not pitch yeast from one brew to the next, as we do in England... But, for my part, I can see no reason to change. Keep everything scrupulously clean, and you can contain the problem; even if you never quite eradicate it.'

Bragg was already at his desk when Morton

came in next morning.

'Working half-time now, are you, lad?' he asked grumpily.

Morton grinned. 'No. But I should mention that Kent are playing Yorkshire, beginning on Saturday. And I am included in the team.'

'Huh! Another three-day holiday?'

'Certainly not less. Yorkshire are always formidable adversaries.'

'Well, while you are working, bend your brains to this. If there is any connection between the Tyrrell lot and the death of Dawson, it is because of this bottom-fermenting business. Mrs Hildred was explaining it to me, yesterday. But I cannot say I understood it properly. The English use a top-fermenting type of yeast; the Germans use a bottom-fermenting type. Both seem content to carry on using their traditional method. But Dawson, no doubt for his own glory, has been trying to get Tyrrell's to switch to bottom-fermenting. He even lectured their board on it.'

'As it happens, I was reading the minutes of that board meeting, last night,' Morton said. 'One cannot, of course, divine the atmosphere of the meeting from such a summary. It baldly stated that Professor Dawson addressed the meeting, and there was some discussion. The board then voted to defer discussion of the proposals to a later date.'

'Was that date specified?'

'No. It could have been a device to sweep the matter under the carpet.'

'Hmm... Interesting. But what I cannot understand is, why kill Dawson over it? It's rather like shooting the messenger because he brings bad news.'

'Indeed! But people do act irrationally.'

'Yes. Why don't we go and prod Eldridge a bit. We have a little surprise for him, after all.'

They strolled along the sunlit pavement towards Bouverie Street.

'Did you see the fair Miss Hildred over the weekend?' Morton asked flippantly.

Bragg frowned. 'Yes. The theatre on Saturday night, and walking in Green Park yesterday.'

'Good! You ought to be able to get your shoes under the bed there!'

Morton expected some equally flippant remark. Instead Bragg sighed. 'I can never fathom women,' he said morosely. 'Why would she want anything to do with the likes of me? Somebody in her position should have been able to pick and choose... I used to think that it was because old Amy is so overbearing put off the young men in their class. I mean, Fanny has got to be desperate, to bear with my company.'

'Why so?'

'You see, Fanny is well educated. She uses words like "mutual dependence" – and that bit was not to impress me. If she even thinks in those terms, she is far above me... So I ask myself, what is it she wants my company for?'

'She might still be able to conceive a child,' Morton suggested. 'There must be considerable wealth in the family, and no ultimate heir in prospect.'

Bragg frowned. 'Yes... You don't want to think in those terms, but you have to. I mean, how could she really want me? Older than her, working class, not worth a shilling.'

'But she may have a genuine affection for you, sir. These things do happen.'

'Maybe... I think this world has gone mad, lad. And not just Miss Hildred, either. Mrs Jenks, this morning... For all the time I have lodged there, I have had the same breakfast. And her husband too, when he was alive. Porridge, three rashers of bacon and two eggs. Every morning except Christmas Day... Suddenly, this morning, she decides it has to change. Away goes one slice of bacon and, in its place, fried black pudding! I ask you!'

Morton laughed. 'And did you eat it?' he asked.

'Well, yes, I did. But when I remarked on it, she said it wasn't black pudding, it was boo dan war. French, you see.'

'*Boudin noir*,' Morton said with a grin. 'The idea of Mrs Jenks providing *haute cuisine* has a certain wry appeal. But did you enjoy it?'

'Well, I suppose I did... And another thing! It seems she and her sister have had a falling out. At the moment she is not for going to live in Southend, after all.'

'They have, of course, a way of dealing with such difficulties in the East,' Morton said straight-faced. 'If the ladies of a Sultan's harem cease to please him, he will have their heads cut off, and start again.'

'You bloody would, too! For me, I just feel like running away.'

'Not before we have solved the Dawson murder, I hope.'

'No... I suppose I am beginning to feel unsettled anyway. In a year's time I shall be retired. A pat on the head and a pension. No function in life; just expected to keep out of the way, while others do the work.'

'Most people look forward to retirement, sir.'

'But not when they are still in their forties.'

Morton grinned. 'I am sure the estimable Miss Hildred could keep you pleasantly occupied for a few years!'

'Huh! Anyway, here is Fortescue & Blount. Get your mind off such nonsense, and concentrate on the case.'

They went into the outer office and rang the bell on the counter. After some moments an elderly clerk appeared.

'Ah! I remember you,' he said accusingly. 'You are the policemen, are you not?'

'Yes. We are the policemen again; and we want to see Mr Eldridge again.'

The man sniffed. 'I will see if he is free,' he said and went out.

Bragg and Morton waited for five minutes and more. A silence seemed to have fallen on the office; not a step, not a voice, not even the rattle of a typewriting machine. Bragg began to prowl up and down. How long would it be, Morton wondered, before he burst out of the room and marched down the corridor in search of Eldridge? But Bragg managed to contain himself until the clerk came back.

'Will you please come this way?' he said.

Eldridge rose from his desk as they entered, and gestured towards chairs. He did not offer to shake hands.

'Good morning, sir,' Bragg said, sitting down. 'Have you found yourself an alibi for the time of Dawson's death yet?'

'I cannot create one, officer,' he said starchily.

243

'No. That would be very remiss, particularly in a solicitor... I am sorry we have had to come back, sir,' Bragg said amiably. 'An investigation into sudden death is a messy business, a bit like a jigsaw puzzle. You cannot fit the bits together, until you can see some sort of overall pattern.'

'I am surprised that you can justify continuing your enquiries, having regard to the outcome of the inquest.'

'Ah, were you there, sir? We did not spot you.'

'No, I was not!'

'I see. Are Fortescue & Blount too high and mighty to soil their hands with criminal cases?'

'It was not that at all.'

'I expect you would have enjoyed it. An open verdict! Sir Rufus Stone was not best pleased.'

'Nevertheless, that was the verdict of the jury, and must be final.'

Bragg tugged at his moustache. 'On the facts before the jury, I expect you are right. But it does not prevent the police from seeing if there are any other facts that bear upon the matter.'

Eldridge sniffed and said nothing.

'In some cases, sir, we can spend weeks poking about, before we find the stray end that unravels it all.'

'Not in this case, I think.'

'No, sir. I suppose we could be criticised for not having found it sooner... Would you take a look at this letter? It was in some papers we took from Dawson's desk.'

Eldridge took the letter and gazed at it.

'That is your handwriting, sir, isn't it?... I know it is not exactly signed, but it does bear the initials J.E.'

Eldridge did not reply.

'Would you like to read it for us, sir?' Bragg said.

'No, I would not!' Eldridge threw it on his desk.

Bragg picked it up. 'Then allow me to, sir; just the important bits... You say: "Unless your liaison with my wife ceases forth-with..." I have never known anybody but a lawyer use that word; but it sounds very forceful. "...ceases forthwith, I will myself take steps to terminate it." Now, this letter is dated the thirteenth of June. It didn't give him much leeway, did it? Not much more than a week later, we find him dead. Murdered.'

'I do not accept that.'

'Well, Professor Burney is convinced of it, and I have never known him wrong.'

'But this is ridiculous! I would not hurt a fly!'

'Not even if it was bothering your wife? No, in view of this letter, I think you would have difficulty in convincing a jury you having been supposedly working alone in your office that afternoon.'

'I never for a moment contemplated physical retaliation, officer,' Eldridge protested. 'I would have moved house to somewhere in the country – travelled in daily.'

Bragg snorted. 'That would hardly have been a wise thing to do,' he said. 'With Dawson accountable to nobody for how he spends his time, it would have given them even more opportunities... I take it you are not thinking of leaving the area in the near future.'

'No, I am not!'

'Good. We don't like locking up lawyers. It discredits the whole judicial system.'

'You can have no conceivable reason for detaining me,' Eldridge said spiritedly.

'No conceivable reason? I can't say that I agree with you there, sir. Not at all!'

Bragg and Morton ran Turnbury to earth in his room at University College.

'You will have seen that the jury returned an open verdict on Professor Dawson,' Bragg remarked.

'I did hear that, yes.'

'May I congratulate you on the way you stood up to the coroner? Sir Rufus can be a bit intimidating, at the best of times.'

'Officials of any kind are loath to face up to unpalatable truths.' His voice was firm and confident.

'Yes. You must have got to know Dawson quite well, when he was your supervisor.'

'Reasonably so, yes.'

Bragg scratched his head. 'You see, in our job, we come up against a lot of ... what is that Latin tag, constable?'

'*De mortuis nil nisi bonum*, sir.'

'That's right. It means speak nothing but good of the dead – on the basis that we shall all be dead one day... Now, you have known Dawson a good long time.'

'Several years.'

'Yes... In your experience, was he always an upright, honourable man?'

Turnbury paused, considering. 'Yes, I believe that he was.'

'And would he be able to set personal considerations aside when judging a colleague?'

'I am sure that he would.'

'So, if he found something not quite right, would he shrug his shoulders and let it go?'

'It would be entirely against his nature.'

'Regardless of the consequences?'

'Absolutely.'

'You see, last month Professor Dawson made an interesting entry in his diary. Why he bothered, who can say? It all seems far too late, since you have got your Master of Science degree, and gone on to higher things. But that entry was to the effect that he had tried to replicate your research results, and failed. We take that to mean he had done what you did in your experiments, and come to a different conclusion.'

'But that is impossible!' Turnbury said forcefully.

'We thought so too. After all, science is the same, whether it's Monday or Friday, whether it's Jack or Jill doing it. That is right, isn't it?'

Turnbury did not reply.

'But then,' Bragg went on, 'we told ourselves that scientists are only human, like the rest of us. And, if a lot turned on the outcome of an experiment, it would only be human to want it to succeed.'

'That should not affect scientific detachment,' Turnbury said.

'No. I am sure you are right. But what if the experimenter is a student, anxious to get on; with his career depending on it?'

Turnbury bit his lip. He suddenly looked young and vulnerable. 'There is something which you ought to know,' he said in an expressionless voice. 'Dawson was an inveterate womaniser. He treated his wife abominably. I became aware of this when he was my supervisor. Mrs Dawson would converse with me, when I was waiting for him at his home... She confided in me, we became close.'

'Close enough to go to bed with her?'

Turnbury flushed. 'I refuse to answer any more questions!' he cried.

'Do you know what I think?' Bragg said quietly.

'I do not care what you or anyone thinks!'

'Well, you should. You could end up with your wrists tied and a hood over your head, walking to the scaffold... I reckon you went to Tyrrell's, knowing he was there. Perhaps you followed him... Anyway, you waited until he was up the ladder, leaning over, filling his little bottles. Then you crept up behind him, hit him on the head with a piece of wood and knocked him into the vat. You started to shove him towards the middle of the vat; then you heard someone coming, and legged it. You might not even have been sure you had killed him. You had to get away before you were seen.'

'That is all fantasy. I was nowhere near the brewery!'

'All right. That will do for now... But don't try to do a runner. We shall have our eye on you.'

After lunch, Bragg and Morton went once more to the brewery. It was beginning to feel almost like a second home, Bragg thought. Men were nodding to them as they passed, even wishing them good day. It would be a good day, Bragg thought, if they could sew up this case; nail Dawson's killer. Turnbury was top of his list – though it did not really make sense. He had an obvious motive; Rosalie Dawson was a luscious bit of stuff. But he had already got from her everything he was going to get ... unless he really thought she might marry him. In worldly terms, it was absurd. She was a woman already in middle age; well preserved, certainly, but going downhill from now on. But young men did not always look to the future; and she was a wealthy woman... Of course, it could go deeper than that. He could have calculated that, once they were married, he could get rid of her; fill his pockets with her money, and spend the rest of his life on the Riviera. He would be wrong, of course, because of the trust. But he would not know that.

'You here again?' George Tyrrell beckoned them into his office.

'We are the proverbial bad pennies,' Bragg said amiably.

'Well, I wish you would turn up somewhere else!'

'I'm sure... You know, sir, our job is a thankless one. We have to poke around – sometimes in corners that are more than a bit grubby. And we are not just looking for facts. We have to try and understand the people involved; why they do what they do.'

'Huh! I should think you know more about this place than I do! You have been here often enough!'

'Young Morton has been going through the company minute-books,' Bragg said.

'I know. Much good may it do him!'

'He has a few questions to put to you, if you don't mind.'

'Fire away!'

'It seems,' Morton began, 'that Dawson was able to experiment here, because you do not practise pasteurism. Yet you are a large brewery, apparently prospering. Why did you elect not to do so?'

Tyrrell narrowed his eyes. 'Money,' he said. 'That is the long and short of it. I have never been in hock to the bank, and I never will. If we had borrowed the money to install pasteurising plant, we would have had the money-men round our necks for evermore.'

'But, Whitbread's did. How could you compete with them thereafter?'

'There is more money behind them than I can call on. But it has cost them! If you take into account the additional interest they have to pay to the banks, I doubt if they are any better off.'

'So you decided – like many other breweries, I am sure – to continue with the old methods.'

'Right. We have to accept that some brews will be spoiled, but not many. Cleanliness is the key to success... And I have to say that Dawson has helped us now and again; tipped us off when these damned coliforms were spreading.'

'So, in a sense, he became part of your team?' Bragg interjected.

Tyrrell's head jerked round. 'No, he did not! Lubbock is our head brewer, and the responsibility lies with him. Everybody else is part of the machinery – even me!'

'There is no need to get hot under the collar,' Bragg said mildly. 'We are only trying to find out why Dawson was murdered.'

Tyrrell frowned. 'That is not what the inquest found, as you well know,' he said.

'The inquest found nothing! An open verdict is ducking their responsibility. No wonder Sir Rufus Stone was furious.' Bragg nodded towards Morton. 'Go on, lad,' he said.

'You invited Dawson to address the board, on one occasion,' Morton said. 'Why was that?'

'Well, he had been in Germany. He came back extolling virtues of specially cultured yeasts... It was a case of an informed amateur interfering in professionals' work. Of course, he was distinguished in his field, so he could not be dismissed out of hand...

He was a strange man. He seemed incapable of taking the long view on anything. If you ask me, the only thing he cared about was his reputation.'

'But that hardly makes sense,' Morton said. 'As we understand it, bottom fermentation virtually precludes the infection of a brew by coliform bacteria. By doing as he suggested, you would have been destroying his natural laboratory.'

Tyrrell shrugged. 'I expect there are other bacteria he could have taken up.'

'So, he recommended switching to bottom-fermenting yeasts?'

'Yes.'

'And the board were prepared to entertain the proposition?'

'Well ... let us say that they might have considered it.'

'So, why did nothing come of it?'

Tyrrell frowned. 'It's like asking me to breach the secrecy of the confessional,' he said. 'Not even the board minutes go into detail.'

'You can rely on our discretion.'

'Huh! Well, you might get a garbled

version from elsewhere, so I have little option... The fact is that the family does not control Tyrrell's brewery any more. We have by far the largest block of shares – something approaching forty-five per cent. But, if all the others ganged up against us, who knows what would follow? They might even get a taste for it!... There is what we might call a natural leader among them, name of Jethro Grainger. We made him a director, to keep him in order. He is a big barley grower in Farnborough, Hampshire. He is able to get us a good price, if we agree to take his barley and have it malted by a concern close to his farm... Now, the other small shareholders tend to follow his lead on anything contentious. So, when he took against Dawson's suggestions, we had no option but to drop them. As I remember it, we did not even proceed to a formal vote.'

'And what had Dawson to say about that?'

Tyrrell frowned. 'I think he must have left the meeting straight after finishing his lecture – for that is what it was. He was certainly not there when we were discussing the matter.'

'I expect he was not best pleased!'

'When we did not adopt his recommendations, you mean? No, that is certainly true.'

'And Lubbock?'

Tyrrell smiled. 'He probably regarded the outcome as a personal triumph!'

'I see. Did Lubbock and Dawson not get on, then?'

'They are both too opinionated for their own good... I suppose that should be past tense, as regards Dawson.'

'So Lubbock will not be sorry that Dawson is no longer preaching at him?'

Tyrrell shook his head. 'I would not quite say that, officer,' he said. 'No.'

7

Bragg and Morton arrived at St George's church, opposite University College, in good time, next morning. They were as interested in who were attending Dawson's memorial service, as in the service itself. As eleven o'clock approached, a cluster of college luminaries formed by the main door. They were mostly wearing black academic gowns and mortar-boards; hoods ranging from black and white, through red to imperial purple. It was not to be an occasion for hiding one's light under a bushel, Morton thought. There was a sprinkling of women in mourning attire. It was a fact of life, that women always had their black dresses to hand. Often, the only time a family assembled as a whole, was at the funeral of a member. And not always the eldest. There were precious few families that had not carried a child's coffin to its final resting place; consigning the hopes of the future to the cold clay.

Bragg nudged him. 'There is Tyrrell – and Lubbock with him. From what they have been telling us, Dawson was more of a pest than anything else. But they have turned up, none the less.'

'See, there is Waller,' Morton said. 'I take it that the young lady on his arm is his fiancee.'

'Ah, yes. What was her name?'

'Lily Simkins. She seems determined not to be over-awed by the occasion.'

'All to the good,' Bragg said gruffly. 'He wants a wife with some backbone, if he is ever to get anywhere. But she will need a thick skin with this lot!'

Through the open door they could hear the organ playing; slow sonorous chords. Catherine Marsden joined them, dressed in sombre colours.

'Has anything happened yet?' she asked brightly.

'No, dear,' Morton said with a possessive smile.

'Oh, dear,' she mimicked him. 'Then I

shall have but little to report!'

'I'm surprised you are bothering, miss,' Bragg said. 'It's not as if Dawson had anything to do with the City.'

'I shall hang my report on the peg of his death at Tyrrell's. After all, the editor did not see fit to reject my report of his death, or my account of the inquest... It is certainly an impressive attendance! Excuse me, I must get some names.' She hurried up the steps and into the porch.

Now a formal procession was assembling in front of the college. A policeman stepped into the tangle of carts and carriages. He eventually brought the traffic to a halt, and shepherded the procession across Gower Street. The man at the head, resplendent in scarlet gown, must be the Vice-Chancellor, Morton thought... They were certainly intent on giving Dawson a good send-off, adulterer or not. But they would not care about marital fidelity. The only thing they set absolute store by was academic integrity. Something which Turnbury had already discarded, if Dawson's diary was to be relied on.

The procession reached the door of the church. There was a deal of doffing of mortar-boards, as its members were swallowed up in the gloom of the church.

'I have not seen Hunt arrive,' Bragg said.

'Nor Turnbury, sir.'

'Well, he is but a lad. Now, Hunt is a man of some standing, and ambitious with it. I am surprised he is not pushing himself forward.'

'Perhaps we ought to go in ourselves, sir,' Morton remarked. 'The church is not large, and I would hate to stand!'

'Huh! You young folk are soft!'

'No. Merely sensible.'

They found seats at the end of a pew, near the back of the church. Bragg made a perfunctory show of praying, then looked about him. It was fairly full, the academics looking very solemn and self-important. The organ was playing Handel's Largo. It always seemed to be trotted out on these occasions; bathing everybody in an atmosphere of solemnity and sanctity. Precisely on eleven o'clock, the final chord reverberated through the church and died away. From the west end a carefully modulated clerical voice announced a hymn, and the congregation stood. The organ played the first phrase of the tune on a quiet reed stop, then began in a firm diapason.

O God our help in ages past...

The black-robed choir processed solemnly down the aisle, their harmony swamped by the assertive baritone of the congregation.

Under the shadow of thy throne
Thy saints have dwelt secure.

Edward Dawson had been no saint, Bragg thought. But security should not be just for saints. If what the parsons said was true, saints needed security less than sinners.

Be thou our guard while troubles last,
And our eternal home.

At the end of the last verse the parson went up into the pulpit, and began an oration. From the way he maundered on,

Dawson had been a paragon of virtue; his life an ideal that everyone present should strive to emulate. It was stupid, irresponsible, Bragg thought, to make out that an ordinary, flawed human being was some kind of saint, just because he had died. It undermined the whole basis of religion, to pretend that people were better than they had really been. There must be scores of people in this church, who had run across Dawson in the course of their careers. They could well know he was a selfish, arrogant pig. After the inquest's open verdict, they might be wondering if somebody had quietly helped him into the next world... Come to think of it he and Morton should have set up a booth in the porch − a sort of confessional, where Dawson's colleagues could have told them what they really thought of him. It would have made a change from the syrupy nonsense the parson was spouting ... But, at last, he seemed to be winding down.

'Not taken from us, but gone before...'

Bragg was damn sure he would never want to join Dawson in heaven.

The vicar came down from the pulpit, and stood at the chancel steps. He said a few prayers, whose import seemed to be invoking divine protection on the college, and everyone connected with it. Then he turned and walked briskly to his vestry. The organ began to play Purcell's Trumpet Voluntary at seemingly breakneck speed. The congregation drifted out of the church. There was general conversation, even subdued laughter. So, what had it all been for? Bragg wondered. It had certainly not been an act of mourning. Perhaps it was no more than an expression of a kind of corporate identity, in the face of adversity.

He dug Morton in the ribs. 'I wonder what our friend Lubbock made of that!' he said.

They went by cab to Waterloo station, and took a train to Farnborough. From the way Lubbock had talked, Bragg thought, Hampshire was at the other end of the earth. In fact, it took them well under an hour to get there. At an inn near the station, they managed to wash down some dry, cold beef sandwiches with a pint of indifferent beer.

The way country folk went on, Bragg thought sourly, townies ate nothing but rubbish; whereas they feasted like lords. Well, they were welcome to this banquet any time. They then went back to the station, where they managed to persuade a surly cab driver to take them to Jethro Grainger's farm.

Grainger was in the yard, watching a farm-hand harness a horse to a cart. He was a well-built man, in his late fifties. He was wearing a twill shirt and riding breeches; his leggings were polished till they shone. A gentleman farmer, Bragg thought sourly. Grainger looked up with a frown.

'City of London police,' Bragg said amiably. 'We gather you are a director of Tyrrell's brewery.'

Grainger nodded.

'And you own a fair slice of the company.'

Grainger frowned. 'I do not want my affairs spread all round the county,' he said sharply.

'Then, perhaps we can go indoors.'

After a moment's hesitation, he beckoned them to follow him. He took them into a

266

low-ceilinged sitting-room. By the look of the beams, Morton thought, the house must be hundreds of years old... Or, at least, this part of it. The other wing was aggressively modern, with its red brick and slate roof.

'Now, what is this all about?' Grainger asked, sitting down opposite them.

'I am sure that you have heard of the death of Professor Edward Dawson,' Bragg said.

Grainger nodded.

'We are making some enquiries into the circumstances of his death.'

'What is there to enquire about over that? He drowned, did he not? A stupid accident! It was always on the cards it would happen. You cannot have amateurs messing about in plant as complex as a brewery.'

'He drowned, yes,' Bragg said equably. 'We are charged, by the coroner, with finding out why he died.'

Grainger frowned. 'I thought that the jury brought in an open verdict,' he said.

'You are well informed, for someone living in the sticks,' Bragg said.

'As a director of Tyrrell's, I have to know these things.'

'Ah, yes. Of course... I gather that you supply a good deal of the barley that is used by Tyrrell's.'

Grainger allowed himself a smile. 'You could say that, yes.'

'And you arrange for that barley to be malted down here.'

'True.'

'I expect you get a commission from the malters, for putting business their way.'

'Now, you know that would be frowned on!'

Bragg smiled. 'Yes... But a man must live.'

Grainger did not reply.

'This Professor Dawson; did you ever meet him?'

Grainger frowned. 'Not more than I had to.'

'Why not?'

'He was a meddler, that's why not!'

'We know he was a very eminent scholar. And we know he was allowed – even encouraged – to carry out research at Tyrrell's brewery. Where was the harm in that?'

'None. I even supported the idea, when it

was first mooted. You know about Pasteur and Whitbread's, I take it.'

Bragg nodded.

'They got nothing but good from it. But the Frenchman was a real scholar; just interested in the pursuit of science, regardless of the outcome.'

'Whereas Dawson...?'

Grainger frowned. 'I am not an academic, so perhaps I should not judge him in that regard. But, in my view, he was interested primarily in promoting himself and his career.'

'But why should that be? He had been a professor for years, and he was still only forty-five.'

'I do not know the why. But I have had a dust-up with him on the how.'

'Is this about his trying to promote bottom-fermenting?'

Grainger looked surprised. 'Yes, it was,' he said.

'We gather, from the minute-book, that his address to the board did not go down well. What we could not understand, is why you were so violently against the suggestion.'

Grainger frowned. 'I baulk at the word violently,' he said. 'I put my views honestly and firmly – which is more than can be said of some others.'

'And, what are your objections?' Bragg asked mildly.

'Up to this point, for well over a hundred years, Tyrrell's have used top-fermenting yeasts. Their whole trade has been built up on it. What they sell, in the main, is traditional draught beer. And they supply it to a large number of public houses, in London and the country to the east and south. They have precious few tied houses... In one sense that is good. If your customer can go elsewhere, it is a powerful reason for giving him what he wants... But Dawson was flying in the face of reason. I am prepared to believe that what he said is sound science. But, where is your business, if you insist on brewing beer that no one wants? You have drunk continental beers?'

'No. I have not had that pleasure,' Bragg said.

'There is no pleasure in it, if you are used to a full-bodied English draught. Lagers are thin and wishy-washy. A half-pint of that, and you would be looking for a pub that sold real beer!'

'So you said that, if it came to a vote, you would see that any change was blocked, one way or another.'

'Yes, I did!' Grainger said defiantly. 'I could not have carried the point at a directors' meeting. But they could not have gone ahead with such an expensive change, without having the shareholders behind them.'

'And you have, I gather, a disproportionate influence on them,' Bragg said with a smile. 'But, of course, it might not have ended there. George Tyrrell seems to have held Dawson in high regard. He might just have let you think you had won the day. He could have been biding his time... You see, it is not quite as simple as both you and he make out. The Tyrrell family still have around forty-five per cent of the shares. It only needs a shade over five per cent to switch sides, for Tyrrell to do what he likes. And it seems that, if Dawson had still been alive, they might just have gone in for bottom-fermenting. For somebody in your position, it could have been an easy solution – to bang Dawson on the head, and drown him in the vat.'

'Rubbish! Look. I admit that I could not survive, as a cereal farmer, without Tyrrell's buying my barley. You have seen the land here – sandy soil over a deep stratum of clay. In the old days, my father would get a good living from it. But now, the prairies of America and Canada are flooding Europe with cheap grain; the market for home-grown cereals has collapsed. Without Tyrrell's I would have to put the land down to pasture; or let the heather grow again, and rent out the shooting.'

'Hmm... So, where were you, on the afternoon of Saturday the twenty-second of June?'

Grainger gave Bragg a level stare. 'I was in London, as a matter of fact,' he said.

'In London, were you?'

'Yes. I am the Liberal party agent in this area. As you know, the Liberal government has just been defeated, over the lack of preparedness of the army. It seemed likely that an incoming Tory government would declare an election, as soon as they acceded to power. The outgoing Prime Minister, Lord Rosebery, wanted to sound out the mood of the party in the shires, before he formally resigned. I was summoned, by telegraph, on Friday the twenty-first of June.'

'Hardly a surprise, was it? So, what happened?'

'For a change, we spoke and the big-wigs listened... Out here, as in all country areas, it is hard to get the voters out. You are not just walking round the corner to the local school, as you are in towns. You have to travel miles, by Shanks's pony, for most people. We, in the country, wanted the Tories to get the blame for calling an election. So we wanted the government to just resign.'

'And, for once, he took your advice, eh?'

'Yes... Not that it will benefit us much. At the election, the Tories will get in by a big majority, I fear.'

'So, is there anyone who can vouch for where you were, on the afternoon of

Saturday the twenty-second of June?'

'I saw a score of people, officer. I am sure that many of them will confirm my whereabouts.'

'Then, if I were you, I would jog their memory, in case they forget.'

'I will... As it happens, I am going up again tonight.' He gave a thin smile. 'If your expenses stretch to first-class tickets, we could even travel together.'

Bragg arrived at Old Jewry next morning, feeling thoroughly jaded. He had got back home, the previous night, to find a message waiting for him. Fanny had decided that she wanted to go to a music hall. But, of course, she could not venture into the East End unaccompanied, so would he call for her? Instead of taking off his collar and tie, settling down with a library book, he had been traipsing all over London. He was just not used to being at somebody's beck and call, once work was over... And, in a year, work would be over for good and all.

'Morning, Joe,' the desk sergeant said cheerfully. 'There was a message for you. I gave it to young Morton.'

'It's good of him to bother to come in,' Bragg said irritably. 'There is only a couple of days to go before he is off playing patball again! What a stupid way to run a police force!'

'You can't deny that lots of bright lads want to join us, rather than the Met, because we have an international cricketer on the muster-roll.'

'More fool them!'

Bragg climbed the stairs to his room. Morton was gazing out of the window. He swung round with a smile.

'Good morning, sir,' he said cheerfully. 'Another beautiful day!'

Bragg grunted, and pulled out his tobacco pouch. He had been late down for breakfast, to Mrs Jenks's obvious disapproval; and he had not had time for his usual pipe.

'I picked up this letter from the desk, sir. The envelope is marked urgent.'

Bragg took it, and slit it open with his pocket-knife. 'It is from Hunt,' he said. 'God Almighty!... He called for Turnbury to go to the memorial service yesterday, and found him murdered! Battered to death, it seems. That has put the cat among the pigeons!' He stuffed his tobacco pouch back in his pocket. 'Come on, lad. We are off to the college!'

By the time it took to find a cab, they could have walked it, Bragg thought irritably. And when they got to the college, Hunt was lecturing. They had to sit fuming in his room until he came back at eleven o'clock.

'It was good of you to let us know about Turnbury,' Bragg said gruffly.

'Have you spoken to the Metropolitan police about it?' Hunt asked.

'No, sir. We do not exactly work hand in glove.'

Hunt raised his eyebrows. 'Are you saying there is rivalry between you?' he asked. 'That would hardly lead to efficient policing.'

'No, not rivalry. We each have our own patch. But ours is right in the middle of the Met's area, like the yolk of a fried egg. So there can be friction, lack of co-operation on both sides. If the truth were known, the Met would like to take us over.'

'I see. Would that not be acceptable to you?'

Bragg laughed. 'It is not the bobby on the street that has the say! It's the men with gold chains round their necks.'

'The Corporation of London, you mean?'

'Yes, sir. And, up to now, they have said no.'

'I see... Well, when I found poor Turnbury, I naturally had the police from the local station called in.'

'Would that be Goodge Street?'

'Yes.'

'Good. Now, can you tell us what happened?'

'Of course.' Hunt frowned. 'I had arranged with Turnbury, the previous evening, that we would walk to church together for Dawson's memorial service. My impression was that he was going to call for me. So I stayed in my room working. As eleven o'clock approached, I began to doubt if my recollection was correct. So I went up to his room...' He swallowed, then took a deep breath. 'I opened the door ... and there he was, on the floor, his head battered into a bloody mess.'

'Was he cold?'

'Not cold, no. Almost normal body heat... But the blood had begun to congeal.'

'So, what did you do?'

'Well, I raised the alarm, of course. One of the college servants went for the police, and I stayed till they arrived. Then they insisted that I should go down to the police station, to make a formal statement. I must say that I found the whole procedure highly distasteful; totally lacking in ... well, in humanity. I began to feel like a felon myself!'

'They are a rough lot, are the Met,' Bragg said. 'But have you any ideas about the crime?'

Hunt frowned. 'None. It seems totally inexplicable. If one looks for a person who might gain from Turnbury's death, one can find no one – at least from an academic perspective. He is on the very lowest rung of the academic hierarchy – a junior lecturer has no security of tenure. Such people are drawn from a relatively large pool of aspiring graduates. It would be impossible to identify specific people on whom his death could confer an advantage.'

'So it was not done for that reason. But it was hardly likely to be the outcome of an academic disagreement, was it? I mean you don't batter someone's head in, over why the sky is blue.'

Hunt smiled. 'Not in the normal course, officer! Indeed, it is totally inconceivable, as you imply.'

'When we heard,' Bragg went on, 'we naturally wondered if there could be a connection with Professor Dawson's death. I mean, they worked in the same field, didn't they?'

'On that basis, I must thank my lucky stars that thermodynamics is about as remote as it is possible to be from Dawson's speciality.'

'But why kill Turnbury? And why then?'

'Well, I hope that you find your answers,' Hunt said. 'Now, I am afraid that I have an appointment ... if there is anything that I can remotely help you with, do not hesitate to ask.'

On leaving the college, Bragg and Morton walked to the Goodge Street Metropolitan police station. The desk sergeant had his tunic off, his sleeves rolled up. Scruffy, Bragg thought, even if it was hot. It would never be allowed at Old Jewry.

'City police,' he said, showing his warrant-card.

'Oh, yes? Are you wanting something?' The tone was cool, but reasonable.

'It looks as if we have interests in common. The lecturer who was found, this morning, in University College.'

'Oh, yes? How are you involved?'

'Only indirectly. A colleague of his, Professor Dawson, was drowned twelve days ago at a brewery in the City.'

'So?'

'We think there may be a connection between the two.'

The sergeant raised his eyebrows. 'Was it the Dawson case, where the jury returned an open verdict?' he asked.

'That's right.'

'Well, that's it, then, isn't it? I mean, your

case is dead. What have you come sniffing round ours for?'

'Our coroner, Sir Rufus Stone, does not regard the Dawson case as closed, whatever the jury found. And the City pathologist is sure it was murder.'

'Then, they made a damn poor fist of it at the inquest.'

'You are absolutely right,' Bragg said mildly. 'Though it was a rogue jury that did the damage, not the coroner's summing-up.'

'And are you looking for us to poke around, and find evidence that will set it right?'

'Not exactly.'

'I am glad of that! What, then?'

'I wouldn't mind glancing through the post-mortem report.'

The desk sergeant pursed his lips. 'You would never get that. It's confidential, you know that. To publish it could influence a jury.'

Bragg bit back the angry retort that rose to his lips. 'Is there no chance of getting hold of it? Just for a few minutes?'

The sergeant was shaking his head, before

Bragg had even finished. 'There is no chance... But one of the detective constables who went to the scene is in. I will see if he is prepared to talk to you.' He turned and went through a door at the rear.

'Hunt was right about one thing, at least,' Morton said.

'What is that?'

'The deleterious effect of non-co-operation.'

'If you mean that being bloody-minded is no help, why not say so?' Bragg retorted, then turned to stare at the notice-board... Definitely the dregs of crime, in the Met area, he thought. Pickpocketing, burglary, keeping a disorderly house. No wonder the City Corporation wanted to keep its own police force.

The door at the rear of the room opened, and a burly young man came in.

'Are you enquiring about the Turnbury case?' he asked Morton with a smile.

'Yes. I am Constable Morton, and this is Sergeant Bragg.'

'Morton? Not Jim Morton, the cricketer?'

'Yes.'

'Crikey! This is amazing! Wait till I tell my son I have met you!'

Bragg cleared his throat. 'We were wondering if you could give us some information on the Turnbury case,' he said firmly. 'Another of the college staff was drowned at a brewery in the City. The coincidence seemed worth looking into.'

The constable shrugged. 'Turnbury was hit about the head with an iron bar. At least, a bloodstained iron bar matching the injuries was found at the scene. Whoever killed him must have gone on hitting him, even after he was dead.'

When they got back to Old Jewry, Bragg flung open the window of his room.

'We need some fresh air on this case,' he said. 'So, where are we?'

'If the two murders are linked,' Morton said with a smile, 'then we can presumably absolve Turnbury.'

'Huh! It's a fine state of affairs when, to prove your innocence, you've got to go and get yourself killed!'

'However, the statistical likelihood of two

academics, at the same institution, being murdered within ten days of each other, in totally unrelated incidents, seems impossibly remote.'

'So they are linked. Then who killed them? Which of our Dawson suspects was in the area at the time?' Bragg asked.

'But we do not know the time of Turnbury's death,' Morton objected.

'All right! Hunt said he was still warm, didn't he?'

'Yes, sir. He also said that the blood had begun to congeal.'

'Very well. So, Turnbury must have come into the college, that morning, otherwise he would not have been there at all.'

Morton grinned. 'I find your logic unexceptional,' he said.

'Stop your piss-taking, lad! I am going step by step. I don't want to miss anything.'

'Very well, sir.'

'But, if he was noticeably cool, by the time Hunt found him ... which was?'

'He said "as eleven o'clock approached". But, if they intended to go to Dawson's memorial service, it must have been very

284

shortly after half-past ten.'

'Yes. Of course, we only have Hunt's word that they did intend to go to the service together... But leave that for the moment. If the blood was clotting by half-past ten, Turnbury must have been killed much earlier... Blast it! We don't know where the body was lying, whether it was clothed, whether the window was open. This rivalry between us and the Met is bloody stupid!'

'We might be able to establish the time he left his home,' Morton suggested.

'Do we know where that is?'

'No. But I suppose the college would tell us.'

Bragg sighed. 'We could, of course, be way off line, in assuming that the murders of Dawson and Turnbury are linked. But let us stay with that idea for the minute. Are there any of our Dawson suspects, that can be eliminated because they could not possibly have killed Turnbury?'

'No doubt enquiries would establish that. But there is one person we perhaps ought to take more seriously,' Morton said.

'Oh?'

'Jethro Grainger. He was in London when Dawson was killed. And he came up to London on our train, yesterday.'

Bragg and Morton were strolling in the direction of Bedford Square. Bragg felt distinctly crochety. They had just paid the earth for a lunch that was long on French names, and short on substance. The West End had gone downhill since he first came to London, he thought. Then you could get a decent steak and fried onions for fivepence. Now they were only interested in toffs with a bag of gold. Of course, in the old days they could have popped into a Metropolitan police canteen, and be welcome. But not any more.

'Perhaps I should tell you,' Morton said, 'that I have decided not to go to South Africa, next winter.'

'South Africa? What the hell are you talking about?'

Morton smiled. 'An England cricket team is to go out, to play three matches in February and March. The selectors have approached me, enquiring if I'd be available.'

'Huh! And what made you turn them down? Your job, or your fiancee?'

'A little of both, perhaps. But, had it been Australia, the challenge would have been irresistible!'

'I would not let Miss Marsden know that, if I were you!'

'I am sure that she would support me in any enterprise I wished to undertake,' Morton said buoyantly.

'Just wait until she has got that plain gold ring on her finger, lad. She will be telling you what you can do, and what you can't do!'

Morton grinned. 'When we are married, she will be able to come too!'

Bragg snorted. 'When I was your age, sportsmen were told to keep away from women; it sapped your strength, they said. No wonder these colonies can knock hell out of us, nowadays.'

'You sound somewhat jaundiced, sir. But, of course, you would have missed seeing the fair Miss Hildred, since we were so late back from Hampshire last night.'

Bragg shook his head. 'It's not quite like

that, lad... Anyway, we are going to the theatre tonight. *A Woman Of No Importance,* at the Theatre Royal.'

'Your beauteous companion will in no sense match the title!'

'Stop piss-taking, lad!'

'Nothing was further from my mind, I assure you, sir.'

'Anyway, we will be back to normal soon. Mrs Hildred has put her foot down, it seems. If Tyrrell's have not made an acceptable offer by this afternoon, the whole thing is off! She has got tickets booked on the two o'clock train to Dorchester tomorrow, so she is serious about it.'

'And the fair Fanny?'

Bragg frowned. 'She will go too, of course.'

'Leaving you bereft?'

'Leaving me behind, anyway.'

'And full of regret.'

Bragg snorted. 'How can you regret something you never had?... To tell you the truth, lad, it will be more like relief. When you reach my age, it is very flattering to have a young woman fussing over you. But there is a fetch to it... I reckon what she wants above all is a child.'

'So, what better than a Dorset grey stallion to father it?'

'Well, I won't deny that part of it would be mightily welcome! But what is the next stage? I am a deal older than she is. I could find myself pensioned off; put out to grass.'

'But, surely you could find a useful niche? What about the brewery? If Tyrrell's do not buy it, you could find a role there.'

'Yes. And that is what it would be – acting. A pretence that I am useful – doing something worthwhile.'

Morton frowned. 'But that is not to be despised. When a policeman plods portentously down the street, he is doing much the same thing. You cannot value him merely on the number of thugs he arrests, and say the rest of his time is wasted.'

'Maybe... But then, there is Mrs Jenks. It was easy when she was going to live with her sister. Now that arrangement is off, I would be letting her down.'

'But you have complained, time and again, about Mrs Jenks's shrewishness!'

'True enough. But she seems to have

changed all of a sudden. I reckon she has had a real falling out with her sister; one that will never be mended.'

'Oh, dear! Families have a propensity for failing one at the most crucial times.'

'Yes.' Bragg pondered for some moments. 'I wonder if Mrs Dawson feels that,' he said. 'Or had she got her insurance policy paid up in advance?'

'You mean Anscombe, sir?'

'Who else, now Turnbury is dead?'

'I wonder if we are being somewhat obtuse,' Morton said.

'Why?'

'Well, we tend to think of her liaison with Turnbury as a rather distasteful yearning for eternal youth.'

'Do we?'

'But suppose that she was behind her husband's death. Suppose that she had motives beyond the merely carnal, for cultivating Turnbury.'

'You mean she got Turnbury to kill her husband, knowing Anscombe was in the wings?'

'Why not? It has a certain elegance, since

she and Anscombe are giving each other alibis for when the deed was done.'

'Hmm... It's possible. And once Turnbury is out of the way, the direct link with Dawson's murder has been destroyed.'

'Indeed!'

'Of course, Anscombe and Mrs Dawson have not yet produced anyone who saw them at the crucial time. Either of them could have done it, without help from Turnbury.'

'Which would relegate him to the category of an untidy loose end in the case.'

'Yes.' Bragg stopped outside Dawson's house. 'Well, she might just be disposed to tell us. Ring the bell, lad.'

The maid acknowledged that her mistress was in, and showed them to the sitting-room. To Bragg, the room seemed subtly different from its appearance at his last visit... There had been photographs of Dawson on the piano; a painting of him in academic robes over the fireplace. Now these were gone; the room seemed lighter, more cheerful. But perhaps it was just the summer curtains.

When Rosalie entered the room, she was still wearing the deep black that would be her garb for a year.

'I did not expect to see you again, officer,' she said with some asperity.

'Oh, we shall keep turning up for a bit,' Bragg said amiably. 'The more we find out, the more we have to check back with what we already know.'

She frowned. 'That is hardly welcome, as you will readily understand. It is painful enough to have to rebuild my life, without the police constantly harassing me.'

'Oh, I would not call it harassing, ma'am,' Bragg said blandly. 'All we want is a civilised chat.'

She hesitated, then gracefully subsided on to the settee.

'It was a very nice memorial service, wasn't it, ma'am?' Bragg began.

She looked perplexed. 'Yes, it was,' she said.

'A good turnout from the college. It must have been a comfort for you, to know how well he was regarded by the other professors and so on.'

292

'Yes.'

'It even got a write-up in the *City Press*. Not many people from outside the City could say as much.'

She smoothed an imaginary wrinkle in her dress and did not reply.

'And what will happen to you now?' Bragg asked in an avuncular tone. 'Have you got family round here?'

'That is a matter I shall consider at the proper time,' she said dismissively.

'Is there ever a proper time?' Bragg said musingly. 'It's a funny word, "proper". I mean, nobody would say it was proper that you would be gallivanting about the West End, or worse, with Charles Anscombe, at the moment when your husband was dying.'

'I had no idea whatever, that he might die that day!'

'So you tell us. And you have a highly respected banker to support your story ... or have you ditched him, for telling us that you were going to bed with him?'

'Charles and I remain good friends,' she said stiffly.

'Good. He was a comfort, I dare say, at the

memorial service... But he would be a good bit older than you?'

'A mere two years.'

'Really! I would have thought it was more. But widowers tend to get sloppy – lose their self-respect... I suppose that is partly what you give him. And, if I may say so, ma'am, you look very smart for a forty-year-old widow. It's to your credit!'

Rosalie frowned. 'I take it that you did not come here to pay me elephantine compliments,' she said acidly.

'What?... Oh, yes, I suppose it does sound a bit clumsy to your refined ears. Yes, Anscombe looks to us to be a very sound chap – a bit dull, but reliable. Would you feel that to be so?'

She cocked her head. 'My feelings for him are a good deal warmer than such a person as you describe would merit,' she said.

'Then you must be hoping our suspicions of him are unfounded.'

'And what, precisely, do you suspect him of?'

'Why, knocking off your husband – or, more precisely, knocking him into the vat of beer and drowning him.'

Her lip curled contemptuously. 'I do not believe that happened, any more than the jury did,' she said.

'That's probably very wise, ma'am. particularly if you intend to marry Anscombe.'

'It is the last thought in my mind, at this moment, officer.'

'Yes... And, of course, you are not in the position most women find themselves in. Tell me, how much was that insurance policy on your husband's life?'

She frowned. 'Insurance policy?'

'Yes. Somebody must have made a claim very smartly. A lawyer from the company turned up at the inquest.'

'What company?'

'The Atlas Assurance Company.'

Her face coloured. 'Ah, yes,' she said. 'Charles did mention it. He prepared the claim for me to sign.'

'I see. And, how much was the sum payable?'

'Five hundred pounds, as I remember it.'

'Hmm. A fortune to most people. But not

to you, I imagine.'

She did not reply.

'Yes,' Bragg said musingly. 'You must have been in something of a dilemma... A pleasant one, that you might have thought you could resolve at your leisure. But now it's out of your hands.'

She forced a smile. 'I have not the slightest idea of what you are talking about!' she exclaimed.

'Well. Here you have been, all these years; wealthy, married to a famous man, a considerable figure in London society. Most women would envy you.'

'Perhaps.'

'But there is often a worm in the apple. And so it was for you. Your husband was a lecher, who would go after any likely bit of skirt. It must have been very wounding for you. After all, it was your money that sustained your sumptuous way of living, not his salary. But he was arrogant and self-indulgent. He must have thought it was his due, if he thought about it at all... Of course, things went as they usually do. You thought it was a game that two could play at. So you found yourself a lover. A mature, wealthy, indulgent lover – Charles Anscombe. Right?'

Rosalie shrugged her shoulders and said nothing.

'Anscombe is a real gentleman, out of the top drawer,' Bragg went on. 'But I somehow doubt if he is a great performer between the sheets. You get an idea about people, in my job; get the measure of them. And I reckon he is fairly cold-blooded, under that gentlemanly exterior. Am I right?'

'I suppose so,' she murmured.

'So here you are; married to a self-indulgent pig, with a lover who can only tickle your fancy now and again... Somehow I don't see you standing for that. And nor did you! All these young men coming to the house for tutorials I don't suppose it was too difficult for you to bump into them in the passage; hold chat with them. And there was one in particular you had your eye on, wasn't there? A lad by the name of Roger Turnbury. Am I right?'

She shrugged. 'Yes,' she said.

'So, while your husband was lecturing,

Turnbury was tupping you in your husband's bed!'

'No!' she cried angrily. 'That is not true... How could we? The servants would have known; and servants cannot be relied upon to be discreet nowadays.'

'Where, then?'

She dropped her head. 'In a City hotel,' she said.

'Which one?'

'The Salisbury, in Salisbury Square.'

'Right. So now you have two lovers and a husband, on the go at the same time. All well and good, you must have thought. And so it was; till your husband found out... He did find out, didn't he?'

She nodded. 'But, in our circle, such an arrangement is not uncommon,' she said tartly.

'I see. Morality is for the masses, is it?... The trouble was that Edward Dawson was not a natural socialite. He resented his wife being poked by any stray mongrel that sniffed her out. So there were scenes - unpleasant scenes. He was not the indulgent husband that your social code required. He was prepared to make a fuss. So he had to be got rid of... I imagine it took you a good long time to work Turnbury up to doing it. But I expect it was not without its pleasures. And I doubt if he was aware that Anscombe was hanging around as well. Anyhow, you finally got your way. Turnbury went over to Tyrrell's brewery, when your husband was taking his samples, hit him over the head and drowned him.'

She was shaking her head slowly from side to side, a dazed look in her eyes.

'He must have thought his luck was in,' Bragg said. 'Because nobody saw him at the brewery. He was able to sneak out, and no one the wiser... Except for Anscombe, perhaps. I reckon he knew about you and Turnbury all along. I would not be surprised if your husband had told him – he was capable of it, to my mind. Anyway, Anscombe wanted you for himself. And here in Edward's place, another rival had appeared. A young rival moreover. Anscombe is an influential man, not used to being crossed in his own world. So he decides to get rid of this pest.'

Bragg paused, Rosalie looking at him apprehensively.

'The body of Roger Turnbury was found in his room at the college, yesterday morning,' Bragg said formally. 'He had been beaten to death.'

Rosalie put her hand to her heart, her face ashen. 'Charles could never have done such a wicked thing,' she said tremulously. 'He is gentle and kind... And there was no need. He knew full well that I would marry him... No! I do not believe it! It would be totally out of character for him to hurt anyone!'

There was a long silence, then Bragg got to his feet. 'I hope, for your sake, that you are right,' he said quietly. 'But, if I were you, I would keep this afternoon's conversation to yourself.'

'Thank you so much for taking me to the theatre, Mr Bragg. I did so enjoy it.' Fanny smiled up at him, as they strolled along Piccadilly to her hotel.

'Me too,' Bragg said warmly.

'I do not understand how Wilde can write so wittily about romantic entanglements between men and women, if he is as unfortunate as the newspapers would have us believe.'

'You mean, being a sodomite? Well, if he isn't, he is indeed unfortunate. He is in prison for it, at this very moment.'

Fanny drew close to him. 'I am glad that you are a real man,' she said.

Bragg cleared his throat. 'So you are having to go back tomorrow,' he said, trying to inject some disappointment into his voice.

'Yes. But I shall have some wonderful moments to remember. And you will be coming to Bere Regis before long.'

'Tell me, miss. What was it that made Tyrrell's drop the idea of buying your brewery?'

'I do not know. Mamma was quite perplexed. By last evening, there seemed to be only a few minor points unresolved. Then a message came to our hotel, this morning, setting today's meeting at three o'clock this afternoon. Mamma thought it was possible that they were holding a board meeting this morning, to finalise the terms of their offer. In the event, George Tyrrell merely informed Mamma that they did not wish to proceed with the purchase.'

'I bet she was livid, after all her work!'

'In part, yes. But I suspect that she was equally relieved.' Fanny smiled up at him. 'Perhaps I ought to be relieved also. Without something to occupy her, she would become restive and irritable.'

'I can imagine that!' Bragg said with a laugh. 'So you will not be travelling abroad, this coming winter.'

'No! It is such a shame! I had set my heart on a month in Monte Carlo. But it is not to be.'

'Well,' Bragg said gruffly, 'you won't have missed much. I can't say I was taken with it.'

'You have been there?' Fanny exclaimed. 'Goodness! You do indeed have hidden depths!'

'It was on a case, so I don't suppose I saw the best of it. But it struck me as a false, shallow sort of place.'

Fanny laughed. 'And thus not at all to the liking of my sturdy, straightforward, English police sergeant!'

'I suppose it was just its foreignness,' Bragg said uncomfortably. 'And me being a peasant in a palace, so to speak.'

There was a silence as they reached the door of the hotel. Fanny stopped and looked up into his face. 'Failing to sell the brewery could prove to be a blessing in disguise,' she said in a soft, insinuating tone. 'There will be a responsible post for you there, whenever you so desire.'

She touched his face with her hand, then turned and walked elegantly to the lift.

8

Bragg arrived at Old Jewry, next morning, to find Morton bustling about, tidying their room.

'Have you got St Vitus's dance, or something?' he said peevishly.

'By no means, sir. After all, it ought to be an auspicious day. Yet, on the other hand, it should be quite the reverse!'

'Stop talking in riddles, lad!'

'If only you had a sense of history, sir!'

'Huh! For the working class, history only goes back as far as your last good dinner.'

'Then, may I remind you that today is American Independence Day... The half of me that derives from my mother wants to cry aloud in rejoicing! On the other hand, my English half bewails the loss of a colony that promises to be the greatest nation in the world.'

'What you should have done, is go to bed

with a bottle of whisky, and stay there till tomorrow.'

'Sound advice, sir! But would it have to be Scotch whisky, or American rye?'

Bragg ignored him and pulled out his pipe. He began to scrape out the bowl with his knife.

'Will you be seeing the elegant Miss Hildred this evening, sir?' Morton asked lightly.

'No, I won't, lad. They are off back to Dorset today.'

'Good heavens! Are you saying that Tyrrell's have broken off negotiations?'

'That's exactly it, though they did not give any clear reason. According to Miss Hildred, her mother went to the brewery, expecting maybe to discuss one or two minor things, then be told Tyrrell's firm offer price. But George Tyrrell walked in, said it was all off, and walked out again.'

'And no reason given?'

'Apparently not... Mind you, I'm not thinking Amy will be heartbroken. I reckon the more she haggled over the value of the business, the more she felt it was worth.'

'Worth to her, you mean?'

'Yes... And yet, at one stage, Tyrrell seemed bent on getting Hildred's. We know that Lubbock reported favourably on it, after he went down to Dorchester. It makes you wonder...'

'About the motivation, you mean?'

'Yes. It may be a bit fanciful. But suppose Tyrrell's lot think we might be on the verge of finding out what happened to Dawson. Something that would knock their reputation, maybe involve people high up in the company. They would not want to be deep in a complicated deal, like buying a brewery. Not till the danger was past... After all, they know all they need to know about Hildred's. They could go down to Dorset with their cheque-book any time.'

'True. Though it would not be wise, even for a concern as big as Tyrrell's, to assume that the redoubtable Amy would entertain their renewed suit.'

Bragg frowned. 'I wonder if we are missing something, lad,' he said. 'Something under our noses, that they think we can't miss.'

Morton shrugged. 'I suppose that any trial

of the perpetrator would put Tyrrell's name in the newspapers. But, so long as none of their staff was implicated in a crime, the publicity could even help their sales.'

'Yes... So they might be thinking it was someone high up in the company.'

'Someone such as Grainger, perhaps.'

'Hmm... I wonder if George Tyrrell knows something we don't know.' Bragg jammed his pipe back in his pocket. 'This case is getting on my nerves,' he said irritably. 'I can't even enjoy a smoke at the moment!'

'And this has nothing at all to do with the departure of the heavenly Miss Hildred?'

'No, it bloody hasn't!... Would Anscombe be at the bank yet, do you think?'

'Who can tell? The senior partner of a gentlefolk's bank must inevitably be a gentleman. Such people like the streets to be aired before they venture forth!'

'Then, if need be, we will drag him out of bed. Come on, lad!'

They had to wait until ten o'clock, for Gosling & Hoare's bank to open. Once more they had to kick their heels in the elaborately decorated banking-hall. But eventually they were shown to Anscombe's room.

'I expect you will know why we are here,' Bragg remarked.

'Since I was in the company of Mrs Dawson last evening,' Anscombe said angrily, 'and since she told me of your quite disgraceful treatment of her, I was certainly expecting you.'

'I see... And yet you have not thought fit to have your solicitor with you.'

'The innocent have no need of lawyers, sergeant.'

'I think,' Bragg said mildly, 'that if I had money in your bank, and I heard you say something as stupid as that, I would be drawing it out damned quick!'

'Then please state precisely what you want of me.'

'Just a chat, at this stage... I take it Mrs Dawson told you about Turnbury's murder.'

Anscombe gave him a level stare. 'Yes,' he said. 'Or, more precisely, she gave me details of certain statements you made concerning his death.'

Bragg raised his eyebrows. 'Are you

thinking that we have made them up?' he asked.

'All I am saying is that suppositions are not facts.'

Bragg nodded his head slowly. 'This is where educated folk have the whip hand of plodders like me,' he said mildly. 'I could not fault a word of what you said. But it doesn't get us anywhere, does it? True, we can only build a case on the facts we establish. But the courts can take a different view. They can come to a verdict beyond reasonable doubt. Do you agree?'

Anscombe nodded reluctantly.

'Now, to me it seems entirely reasonable – Dawson being the pig he was – that Rosalie Dawson should turn to you for support and comfort. And, when you had got to the stage of bedding her, you could perfectly naturally have thought of ways you could make it permanent... Have you found anybody yet, who could swear they saw you shopping in the West End? A bill in your pocket for something you bought then?'

Anscombe dropped his gaze. 'No,' he said.

'Right... You see,' Bragg went on

confidingly, 'we can understand how you feel about Rosalie. I reckon I would have thought he was not fit to lick her shoes... Of course, plenty of people would have just run off together – particularly in London society. Put two fingers up at the notion of propriety, and made a new life together. But that was difficult for you, wasn't it? I mean, you are the head of an important bank. If you can't be trusted with other people's wives, how can you be trusted with other people's money? So you decide that your only option is to get rid of Dawson.'

Anscombe shook his head, but said nothing.

'You know your way about Tyrrell's brewery,' Bragg went on. 'Rosalie could have told you when Dawson was going to be there. Once he was up the ladder, it was easy. Creep up behind him, hit him on the head with a piece of wood, and shove him into the vat. Why did you not push him fully into the vat, sir?'

Anscombe looked at him coldly. 'These are your fantasies, sergeant, not mine,' he said.

'I reckon it was because you heard someone coming, and were afraid you would be recognised.'

'If an assailant were in the old vat house, and heard footsteps approaching, he would be trapped,' Anscombe said. 'There is no way out but the one passage.'

'So you do know your way around that part of the brewery?'

'Of course! In common with scores of notables, I have been shown around *ad infinitum*. If you regard that as an indication of guilt, you will have to spread your net very widely indeed!'

'Yes... I can see the force of that, sir. But things have moved on a bit now, haven't they? Young Turnbury has been murdered now. A frenzied attack it was. Whoever did it must have been near out of his mind. They say the murderer must have kept on hitting him, even after he was dead.'

'And, who is this Turnbury?' Anscombe asked perplexed.

'One of Dawson's acolytes – recently made a junior lecturer.'

'Murdered? But how can you remotely

think that I was connected with such a crime?' Anscombe exclaimed. 'I did not even know the man!'

'You had heard about him, though?'

'Only from your mouth, officer. When was he killed?'

'Tuesday morning. In his room at the college.'

'I have not the remotest idea where that would be, sergeant. But even if I did, the chances of a complete stranger being able to wander about University College undetected seem to me infinitesimal.' He reached over and pressed a bell on his desk. 'I now have an appointment with clients,' he said. 'In the unlikely event that you need to see me again, please get in touch with my secretary.'

The door opened, and a young man appeared.

'These people are just leaving, Perkins,' Anscombe said firmly. 'Please show them out.'

'You know, lad,' Bragg said, when they were once more in the street, 'it's one of the pleasures of this job – tweaking the noses of the rich and powerful, and being able to get away with it!'

'Perhaps. But you must realise that the mongoose does sometimes get bitten by the snake.'

'But that is why I have you tagging along. You look too healthy and honest to be party to my skulduggery... And now, I have a mind to call on our friend Eldridge. No one could accuse us of trying to mislead a lawyer, could they?'

'But Eldridge is in a different category from Anscombe,' Morton objected.

'Agreed. He is one of our cuckolds, not one of our lechers.'

'Yes.'

'You are not thinking that Turnbury's death has eliminated Eldridge, are you?' Bragg asked.

Morton frowned. 'I suppose that I am.'

'In this game, you have to learn to keep all the balls in the air at once. After all, it could be that Turnbury was killed while tackling an intruder.'

'I suppose so. It would seem that I am

trying to impose a symmetry on the facts, that may not exist.'

'A fatal mistake, lad. And we want it to end up being fatal for the murderer... Here we are, Bouverie Street.'

They went into the offices of Fortescue & Blount. The white-haired clerk was still behind the reception desk. From his rumpled clothes, Morton thought, he might never have been home since their last visit.

'Is Mr Eldridge in?' Bragg demanded.

The man hesitated. 'Well, he is in the building, but...'

'I want to see him,' Bragg interrupted curtly.

'Am I right in thinking that you are the gentlemen from the police?'

'Apart from the gentlemen bit, that's right.'

The clerk gave him a reproachful glance, then went out.

They waited for something approaching ten minutes. At one point, a good-looking young woman poked her head round the door, and asked if she could do anything for them. Bragg shook his head irritably, as if a ribald rejoinder had not even flitted through his mind. Eventually the clerk returned and ushered them into Eldridge's room.

'Sorry to turn up without an appointment, sir,' Bragg said amiably. 'But you know how it is.'

Eldridge frowned. 'No, I do not know how it is!' he replied irritably.

'Well, in this job we keep digging up facts; have to try and relate them to what we know already; build a picture out of them... How is Mrs Eldridge?'

'If you must know, sergeant, a considerable rift has developed between me and my wife.'

'It's understandable,' Bragg said equably. 'I take it you are satisfied she and Dawson were lovers?'

'"Satisfied" is an inapt word, in the circumstances.'

'No doubt. But what surprises us is that you claim not to have known about it.'

Eldridge sighed. 'Once you had brutally compelled me to face the facts, I realised that I had suspected something of the sort. Caroline is an independent, self-willed woman. But I should have realised that even she would not set off, alone, to visit an aunt in a sanatorium in the south of France.'

'She went with Dawson, did she?'

'Not to Grasse, no. But with Dawson to Florence, certainly.'

'Yet you still say you didn't kill Dawson.'

'Of course. It happens to be true. Indeed, I am astonished that your enquiries are continuing, in view of the verdict of the coroner's jury.'

'Ah, yes. But you, being a lawyer, would know how little weight we need attribute to that. Were you at the inquest?'

'No. I had better things to do.'

'Well, between ourselves, Professor Burney is convinced Dawson was murdered. So you must be high on our list of suspects.'

'But not the only name, I would suppose.'

'That is true, sir.'

'Well, if it is of any relevance to you, I can say that my wife and I have discussed the events, and we are settled on the way forward.'

'All lovey-dovey eh?'

'No. But we have agreed on a *modus vivendi* which may, in time, repair the damage.'

'Good!' Bragg mused for a moment, then, 'Does the name Roger Turnbury mean anything to you?' he asked.

Eldridge frowned. 'I have a feeling that I should know the name, but I cannot place him.'

'At Tyrrell's. One of Dawson's minions.'

'Ah, yes. I have certainly heard of him.'

'But not met him?'

'I am not aware of having met him.'

Bragg snorted. 'That is a careful, lawyer's sort of answer,' he said.

'Thank you, sergeant.'

'And where were you on Tuesday morning?'

'The second of July?'

'Yes.'

Eldridge took out a pocket diary, and flicked through the pages. 'At what time on Tuesday morning?' he asked.

'Any time between seven and ten o'clock.'

'I was in Bristol in connection with the purchase of a factory building. My client and I stayed in the Grosvenor Hotel, having travelled down the previous evening.'

'And the name of this client?'

'Michael Nairn of Aldersgate Street, here in the City. He is a manufacturer of linoleum, and is expanding his business. If you felt it necessary, I am sure that he would confirm what I have told you.'

'Very well, I may do that, sir... By the way, I gather that the negotiations for Tyrrell's to buy Hildred's brewery have broken down.'

'That is the case.'

'Any particular reason for that?'

Eldridge gave a sly smile. 'You mean, any reason in which the police might legitimately be interested?

'If you like.'

'Well, you could get the bones of it from the minute-book anyway... The board was split over the affair. I suspect that Lubbock was the driving force in the project. No doubt his stature would have been increased considerably, as the chief brewer of the combined businesses. And one imagines that the expansion would not have stopped there. However, there was a shareholders' meeting, first thing yesterday morning. There was a good deal of opposition from the smaller shareholders. It became apparent that, on a vote, the proposal to buy Hildred's brewery would be defeated. So the proposal was dropped.'

'Just like that? After all that time and effort?'

'Indeed, sergeant. And I would have advised nothing less. In my experience, board-room feuding can ruin a business more certainly than any other cause save insolvency.'

'And, is there no chance of the proposal being revived?'

Eldridge pursed his lips. 'I would say not. Knowing my clients as I do, I would think it in the highest degree unlikely.'

Bragg and Morton walked in silence to Waterloo station. For once Morton could not fathom the sergeant's mood. He wondered if it had more to do with the Hildred situation than the Dawson case. He tried to put himself in Bragg's position. He had certainly achieved his potential in the police force; was, in fact, a formidable detective officer. But to be left a widower, after such a short period of marriage, would have destroyed the confidence of many men; left them feeling ostracised, defeated. It could explain his sudden outbursts of anger, of petty irritation even. Morton wondered how he would survive that experience; if his own marriage to Catherine were to be cut short so cruelly... Of course, Sergeant Bragg did not have many options. He could have become a clerk, or gone to work on the land. Morton realised, with wry amusement, that his own options were remarkably similar.

'You are quiet, for a change,' Bragg remarked accusingly.

'I was thinking about Dawson, sir. How one man's arrogance could produce so much destruction and heartache.'

'An arrogant bugger, he was, and no mistake. It's queer, isn't it. Both of us reckon he deserved what he got, ten times over; yet we are spending our time trying to catch the sod who did it.'

'Straining every sinew in the quest,'

Morton added lightly.

'Yes... I wish I was more sure about the Turnbury side of it, though. I mean, it might have no connection whatever with Dawson's murder. I sometimes think that, if we were on the outside looking in, we would say: "Those two silly buggers are wasting time that could be better spent." It makes me uneasy, lad.'

'But you have the Commissioner's support.'

'Not for much longer, I think. Inspector Cotton cornered me, last night. Wanted to know what progress we are making, and so on. I couldn't tell him it was no business of his, could I?'

'So, what did you say?'

'I suddenly remembered that he is the liaison officer with the Met. So I told him about the Turnbury murder; how you, lad, were convinced it was linked to Dawson's death.'

'Thank you so much, sir!'

'Which is basically why we are now going down to see Turnbury's parents. I mean, to disregard his suggestion would be putting up two fingers with a vengeance.'

'But, suppose that the Met have been down to see them already?'

'You will have to flannel your way out of it, won't you, lad. That's what we keep you for.'

They had a snack lunch in Waterloo station, then caught a train to Guildford. Once there they took a rather decrepit growler to the village of Burpham.

'I don't know where they get these names from,' Bragg grumbled, as they clip-clopped along. 'They will be having Belcham and Fartham before long!'

Morton put his head out of the window. 'There is a village ahead,' he said. 'I assume that it must be our goal.'

'Right, lad. Now is your chance to show me how it should be done.'

The village was no more than a huddle of houses around a village green. Telling the cabby to wait for them, they strolled over to a general store. It was no shakes as a business, Bragg thought. A few bits of crockery, cleaning materials, some enamel pans. Of course, out here, in the country, people would grow their own vegetables.

The butcher, across the road, would supply them with meat, they would bake their own bread... It ought to have been a heart-warming thought. But he had been brought up in just such a village. He knew how stultifying it would be.

'Good morning, ma'am,' Morton was saying in his upper-class voice. It was odd how she reacted, Bragg thought. Her bright smile, her eagerness to please. In an area like this, they would touch the forelock for evermore... Now her face was solemn, her mouth pursed. Terrible doings in London... What was Turnbury wanting with university education, anyway? It was almost his parents' fault. Eventually Morton wormed out of her the location of the Turnburys' house. It proved to be a detached stone building, set in a large garden. A wreath of greenery and flowers was tied to the front door with black ribbon. The curtains were drawn at the windows.

Morton knocked on the door. For some moments nothing happened. Then a middle-aged man came round from the back of the house. He looked from the growler to the policemen in surprise.

'I thought you were ... bringing Roger back,' he said plaintively. 'It was supposed to be this afternoon.'

'We are not from the undertakers,' Morton said gently. 'We are police officers.'

'Oh! I was wondering when you would get around to doing something,' Turnbury said waspishly. 'You had better come in.'

They followed him along the path to the back of the house, and into a big kitchen. A woman dressed head to toe in black rose as they entered.

'They are policemen,' her husband announced bleakly.

'Oh.' She sank back into her chair.

'Your son was helping us with some enquiries,' Morton said gently. 'He was a very clever scientist, and he was able to explain to us what Professor Dawson was doing, when he was killed.'

'And now it is Roger!' she wailed, dabbing at her eyes.

'I am so sorry. But we will catch his killer, never fear.'

'That will not bring him back!'

'I know. But, at least, an evil man will pay for his crimes.'

'Crimes?' Mr Turnbury echoed.

'We believe that the same man who killed Dawson, also murdered your son.'

'So, if you had done your job properly, our son would still be alive!'

Morton decided to back-pedal. 'I do not believe that the crimes were directly connected,' he said. 'Rather that they had a common causation.'

Turnbury looked at Morton uncertainly. 'Well, Roger's killer must be caught and hung. So we have got to help you, haven't we?'

Morton nodded. 'We would like to look through any papers that he might have here,' he said. 'It is possible that they might give us a lead.'

'Come on then.'

Turnbury took them up two flights of stairs, to a gloomy landing at the top of the house. He opened a door. 'This was his bedroom when he lived here,' he said. 'As you can see, he still kept books and papers here. He would come and see us every second week, and do a bit of work on his sideline.'

'Sideline?' Morton asked.

'He had a little business, that he ran from here. He said that he would not have been able to pay his way without it.'

'What kind of business?'

'Oh, laboratory equipment and so forth. He used to supply schools and small factories with what they needed. He was going to give it up, when he got his senior lectureship.'

'I see. We did not find any records relating to this business in his college room,' Morton said.

'They are kept here.' Turnbury opened a drawer in a chest by the bed, and took out two account books held by a canvas strap. 'Will you want to take them away?'

'Perhaps. But I may have time to glance through them here.'

'Right.' Turnbury hovered uncertainly. 'Will you be needing me?' he asked.

'No, sir. And I am sure that you would prefer to be with your wife.'

'Thank you.' He nodded and went out of the room.

Morton turned to Bragg. 'I think you ought to take over the tiller now, sir,' he said.

'Right, lad. What we are looking for, is anything that connects him with Dawson; correspondence, notes he might have made on research matters... Use your head. And, if there is anything you cannot understand, we take it back with us. Somebody somewhere will explain it to us.'

Bragg picked up the account books and released the strap. He pored over them for some time, then turned to Morton. 'Have you had any luck?' he asked.

'No, sir. I have gone through every drawer. I have examined every book on the shelves, in case a loose paper might have been tucked away there. I fear that I have drawn a blank.'

'Hmm... This sideline of young Turnbury's seems to be quite remarkable. As to the records, any accountant would throw up his hands in horror at them! He only has two books; a cash book, and what we might call a goods in and out book... Are you sure there is no correspondence around?'

'Merely orders from clients.'

'Well, come and look at this ledger. We have details of goods sent out to customers and there is only a handful of them; schools and works laboratories, as his father said. On the opposite page there is a record of incoming stock. Oddly enough, there is no reference to the name of the supplier; though that would not be significant in itself. You would expect to pick that up in the cash book.'

'Right.'

'Now, when we turn to the other ledger, we find that it is indeed a cash book... Look, on this side is money received for goods sold, with the name of the customer against each entry. But there is never an entry for cash paid out! I'll tell you what, lad. I wouldn't mind a sideline like this myself!'

'But the cash received is presumably real. So it must have been paid to Turnbury for real goods.'

'Right. The question is, who bought them in the first place?'

'Clearly not his parents. Interestingly enough, I have seen no invoices for goods inward; no correspondence relating to them.'

Bragg nodded. 'Keep going, lad.'

'I confess I am floundering, sir.'

'Perhaps that's not altogether surprising, in somebody who has never had to count his pennies... We agree that these goods have been coming from somewhere. Turnbury has not paid for them; there is no evidence here that he ordered them. So can you think of an organisation that uses laboratory equipment, and that is so big and dis-organised it doesn't know what it has received and what it has not?'

'University College could well fit the bill, sir.'

'Clever lad! Almost as clever as Turnbury. I reckon he has an understanding with someone in the office there. Turnbury gets orders here, that are sent in by schools and what not. He passes them on to his accomplice at the college. The goods are sent here; the college unwittingly pays for them. Then Turnbury sends the goods to his customers and collects the money for them.'

'Do you think this might have been the

reason for his death?'

'I suppose it might. If so, it is no concern of ours. And I am damned if I will drop it into the Met's lap. Let them do their own leg-work!'

'So, have we achieved anything by coming here?'

'Did you find anything relating to Turnbury's work at Tyrrell's? Any mention of Dawson?'

'No, sir.'

'Then, yes, we have drawn a blank. But, at least, we are aware of it now. And we know that Turnbury was a wrong-un.'

'But, nevertheless, out of our jurisdiction.'

'Unless we can find a link with Dawson's murder.'

They took their leave of the Turnburys, and the cab carried them back to Guildford. They had ample time for a cup of tea at the station before their train pulled in. Morton sat by the window, and took Dawson's desk diary from his pocket. By now he felt he had some idea of how an Egyptologist felt, when trying to decipher hieroglyphs. He had now worked his way through it, from the beginning of the year to the end of May, without finding anything new that was remotely comprehensible. He turned to June the first. At least there were some whole words here.

W Eureka!
Saccharomyces cerevisiae var. dawsonianus
? Saccharomyces cerevisiae dawsonianus

He turned the remaining pages, but found no further lapses into intelligibility.

Once they were back in Old Jewry, Morton showed the diary to Bragg.

'Apart from Dawson's comments on Turnbury, this is the only entry remotely decipherable, in the whole diary,' he said. 'Why would he make it *en clair?*'

'On what?' Bragg asked irritably.

'Not in code.'

'Perhaps to amuse some over-educated bugger like you!'

'No. I am sure that it must be important. The last word in each case, clearly refers to Dawson himself. And, more significantly, *eureka* is Greek for "I have found it".'

'Found what?'

'Some new bug or bugs, perhaps.'

'So Dawson was seeing that he got the credit for that.'

'Indeed! And not unreasonably, After all, that is how an academic reputation is built.'

'Yes... Yet I have something niggling away at the back of my mind. Here! Give me those interview notes.'

He took the file and began to leaf through the papers. 'Why the hell does education have to affect people's writing?' he asked irritably. 'Your scribble is damn near as indecipherable as Dawson's code... Bloody hell! I remember now. Where is my notebook?... It was on the day of the murder. You were playing pat-ball... Here we are. I went in search of Waller, to get some background. He was telling me about wort-spoilers. He was explaining that Dawson was researching bugs; but he himself was interested in wild yeasts. He said that brewers' yeasts all belonged to the one family – of plants, I gather. And he used those two words.'

'*Saccharomyces cerevisiae?*'

'Yes. I couldn't write it down, naturally, being a complete ignoramus. But I remember it well enough.'

'So that explains everything,' Morton said exultantly. 'It was Waller who made this discovery, and Dawson intended to take the credit for it; pass it off as his own!'

'But Dawson could not just have stolen the discovery. Waller would have exposed him... So he would have to get rid of Waller. Where do you think he would be, at this time of day?'

'If we waited at his lodgings, we would be certain to find him sometime.'

'Right... Bowling Green Lane, isn't it?'

'Yes, sir. Number three.'

'I remember now. I went there on the day of the murder, but Waller was not there. This young woman answered the door. Crying, she was. It seemed odd at the time... I wonder. Get us a cab, lad.'

The evening traffic was heavy, as their hansom made its slow way westward. In the end Bragg paid off the cab at Smithfield, and they began to walk. Morton suspected that he was blaming himself for not having made an arrest earlier. But no one had been harmed by the delay – unless Turnbury had been involved in some way. When they reached Bowling Green Lane Bragg slackened his pace.

'Miserable sort of place, isn't it?' he said gruffly. 'No wonder people fight against the system that puts them here.'

He knocked at the door of number three, then turned away to look down the street.

There came the noise of the door being opened. 'Yes?' A young woman's voice.

Bragg faced her. 'We were hoping to have a few words with David Waller,' he said.

She smiled. 'He has only just come in.' She looked at Bragg. 'You have been here before, haven't you? Do you know where his room is?'

'No.'

'Up the stairs. First on the left.'

'Thank you, miss.'

Bragg knocked on Waller's door and went in. The room held the bare minimum of furniture. There was a threadbare carpet surrounded by patterned fawn linoleum. A bed was in one corner; a table and a chair under the window. There was not an ounce of comfort in the place, Bragg thought. Waller himself was standing by the table, a book in his hand.

'Hello, son,' Bragg said quietly. 'I thought it was time for another chat.' He crossed over and sat on the chair.

'I am surprised that there is anything to chat about, sergeant,' Waller said in an aggrieved tone.

Bragg nodded. 'You could be right about that. But we have to hear your side of things.'

Waller frowned. 'My side of things?' he exclaimed. 'What things?'

'Well, primarily Dawson; though if you have any thoughts on Turnbury, we would be interested to hear them.'

'This is madness!' Waller exclaimed. 'You are out of your mind, if you think that I had anything to do with the death of either of them!'

'Yes. Well, I grant you there were more obvious candidates. A clutch of aggrieved husbands, a couple wanting Dawson's wife for themselves. We went off on a false scent at the start... In fact, you hardly put a foot wrong. Our trouble throughout has been the sheer number of suspects,' he mused, 'what with both Dawson and his wife treating the marriage bond somewhat lightly. And yet, in itself, infidelity was not a very strong peg to hang a murder charge on. Since everybody was enjoying themselves in what passes for a civilised fashion, where was the point in breaking it up? Much the same situation was to be found at the college. We could make out a case for Dawson's death being advantageous to various people. But there was no guarantee that any single individual would profit by his death. So motive as a driving force was not very helpful. And when we considered opportunity, there were scores of people who knew their way around Tyrrell's, so could have tipped him in the vat. And yet, Professor Burney was adamant that Dawson had been murdered.'

Waller was staring fixedly at Bragg, hands clenched.

'I expect you thought you had got away with it,' Bragg went on. 'That inquest verdict muddied the water. Any other coroner might have shrugged his shoulders, and left it there. But not Sir Rufus Stone! He was adamant that our investigation should continue. And he was right, of course... And yet it was difficult to find a strong enough motive. On the means and opportunity fronts, you started off as a prime candidate; but it was difficult to see what you could possibly gain by Dawson's death. Indeed, you cleverly got us to believe that you would lose by it.'

'That is still true!' Waller burst out. 'I did not kill Dawson!'

'Oh, yes, you did.' Bragg said quietly. 'Indeed you had to be one of only two real suspects. Only you and Turnbury really had the knowledge of the brewery that was needed – short of the people actually working there. And none of them had a motive.'

'Nor had I!'

'Well, we thought that too, at first. It seemed that you could only lose by his death... And, to be honest, you don't really look the murdering type. But, of course, at bottom he was a ruthless, unprincipled man. It is interesting, the number of people not intimately connected with Dawson, who said he was willing to sacrifice anybody, if it would enhance his reputation. I expect you would feel the same.'

Waller did not respond.

'It was bad luck, really. We had our suspicions about you, but we could not put flesh on the bones, so to speak... Until we found Dawson's diary. That was where you went wrong; though how you would have got hold of it, I cannot imagine. But, when we read it, everything fell into place.'

Waller snorted, lip curled.

'Yes, it did! Because there, as plain as a pikestaff, was his plan to steal your discovery... If your counsel, at the trial, plays on that, I wouldn't be surprised if you cheat the hangman. I mean, a new strain of yeast was not even in his area of research. I reckon every man jack of the jury will put himself in your shoes.'

Waller was staring into the distance. There was a silence; then he spoke in a tired, spent voice.

'He left me no choice,' he said. 'It was my discovery. He had not the remotest claim to it. It was not in his field; he only knew of it because he was my supervisor. But he had to be the only luminary in the natural sciences department at the college... And he was already head and shoulders above everyone else. Yet he had to have more...' Waller paused. There was silence for a space; then he began again.

'He promised that, if I would abandon my claim to the discovery of that yeast variant, he would use his influence to get me preferment at University College. He then threatened that, if I did not agree to his plan, he would make sure that I never held a university post anywhere... I agreed to meet him at Tyrrell's, that Saturday afternoon. I think he felt it was safer – more discreet – than having a discussion at the college.'

'So what happened?' Bragg asked quietly.

Waller took a deep breath. 'Dawson had come equipped for taking samples from the vat. Whether that was merely a blind, I cannot say. Anyway, he mounted the shorter ladder, with one of his bottles. I reared the longer ladder at the vat and climbed up close to him... I have thought about this endlessly. It was all so grotesque... But I really believe that his own line of research was petering out.'

'You mean, into bugs?'

'Yes. It seems absurd, I know. But the proposition that he put to me, was that I should make available to him all my material on wild yeasts. In return, he would become my mentor; would see that, within the shortest time possible, I was made a junior and then a senior lecturer. I would then have security of tenure as a teacher in a prestigious seat of learning; that was how he put it... He was leaning over the vat, filling one of his little bottles. Confident that he could bend me to his will... I do not really remember what happened. I had an intolerable feeling of revulsion. He looked up at me, with contempt in his face... The next moment I was hitting him. I do not remember picking up the piece of wood – but there he was, face down on the surface. I tried to push him further into the vat, but he was too big and unwieldy. And I had to save myself! So I got down the ladder, picked up Dawson's equipment, and crept away.'

'There is one thing that I do not understand,' Bragg said quietly. 'Show him the entry in Dawson's diary, constable.'

Morton took it over to Waller, open at the relevant page.

'Those two lines of scientific jargon,' Bragg said. 'They are identical, except that in the second the word "var." is left out.'

Waller looked at it, and his lip curled in contempt. 'The first line is the correct technical description – or would have been, had Dawson made the discovery. A variant of *Saccharomyces cerevisiae*.'

'So, in the second line,' Morton suggested, 'he would have been laying claim to a whole clan, rather than one new member of it.'

'If you like.'

'But it really ought to be *Saccharomyces cerevisiae*, var. *wallerensis*?' Morton remarked.

'Yes.'

'Why then, did he put the second entry,

with the question mark and no "var."?'

Waller's lip curled with contempt. 'Dawson was always trying to get away from Pasteur's shadow. And Pasteur omitted the "var." on one occasion. In a man of genius it was tolerable, but...' Waller shrugged.

There was a silence, then: 'We heard mention of a young woman thereabouts, at that time,' Bragg said.

Waller dropped his head. 'It was my girl friend, Lily Simkins... We had let our feelings run away with us. The doctor had just told her that she was pregnant. She came to tell me.'

'God Almighty! What a mess!' Bragg exclaimed. 'Left to me, I reckon I would tell you to bugger off to America... But what about Turnbury?'

Waller gave a sneering laugh. 'He was too clever by half! He guessed that I had been involved in Dawson's death. He has always looked down on me... He thought he could amuse himself at my expense. I knew he would be going to the memorial service, so I went to his room. He made a remark – about everyone else but me, being at the service to thank God for Dawson's life... I knew he would carry on in that strain. But I was ready for him. I had an iron bar with me. So I shut his mouth for good and all!'

A silence fell on the room; an emptiness, as if the emotion of the encounter had drained away. Finally Bragg stirred himself.

'David Waller,' he said, 'I am arresting you for the wilful murders of Edward Dawson and Roger Turnbury. Get your coat; you are coming with us.'

'You are back late, Mr Bragg! I thought you said those Dorset people were going home.'

'They have done, Mrs Jenks,' Bragg said wearily. 'The truth is, I've had a bad day. You know, in this job you sometimes hope against hope that things will turn out differently. But they never seem to.'

'I did think, after supper, we might go up to the Rose and Crown,' Mrs Jenks said with a smile. 'I'm all changed, ready.'

'You look very nice, Mrs Jenks.'

'And I've got you something special for your supper, too!'

'All your cooking is special,' Bragg said warmly.

'But I got it out of a book! It's what they eat at the Reform Club... They call it carpet-bag steak – though it's much posher than it sounds.'

'Really? I expect it's a bit complicated, then!'

'No!' Her face was glowing. 'All I did was buy a nice thick piece of steak, cut it along the middle, and stuff it with oysters!'

'It sounds very upper-class!'

'Well, why not? I thought. I can afford to get us something special now and then.'

'And a bottle of beer will go down very well with that – as long as it isn't Tyrrell's!'

'It won't take long to cook ... Or shall I leave it till tomorrow?'

Bragg smiled. 'No, Mrs Jenks,' he said. 'I reckon we can allow ourselves a celebration tonight!'

The publishers hope that this book has given you enjoyable reading. Large Print Books are especially designed to be as easy to see and hold as possible. If you wish a complete list of our books please ask at your local library or write direct to:

Dales Large Print Books
Magna House, Long Preston,
Skipton, North Yorkshire.
BD23 4ND

This Large Print Book for the partially sighted, who cannot read normal print, is published under the auspices of

THE ULVERSCROFT FOUNDATION

Other DALES Titles In Large Print